ON
ICE

ON ICE

A NOVEL

RED EVANS

LARGO, USA

O N   I C E

For information, contact Kunati Inc., Book Publishers in both USA and Canada.
In USA: 6901 Bryan Dairy Road, Suite 150, Largo, FL 33777 USA
In Canada: 75 First Street, Suite 128, Orangeville, ON L9W 5B6 CANADA,
or e-mail to info@kunati.com.

F I R S T   E D I T I O N

Designed by Kam Wai Yu
Persona Corp. | www.personaprinciple.com

ISBN-13: 978-1-60164-015-4   ISBN-10: 1-60164-015-3
EAN 9781601640154   FIC000000 FICTION/General

Published by Kunati Inc. (USA) and Kunati Inc. (Canada). Provocative. Bold. Controversial.™

h t t p : / / w w w . k u n a t i . c o m

TM—Kunati and Kunati Trailer are trademarks
owned by Kunati Inc. Persona is a trademark owned by Persona Corp.
All other trademarks are the property of their respective owners.

Library of Congress Cataloging-in-Publication Data

Evans, Red.
  On ice : a novel / Red Evans. -- 1st ed.
    p. cm.
  Summary:"A road story novel based on a news story in which a young boy, a
banjo player and a flatulent dog accompany the corpse of a fiddler in a
Studebaker pickup from West Virginia to Louisiana"--Provided by publisher.
  ISBN-13: 978-1-60164-015-4
  ISBN-10: 1-60164-015-3
  I. Title.
PS3605.V374O52 2007
813'.6--dc22
                    2007028102

DEDICATION

To Charles H. Evans

Acknowledgements

One Sunday afternoon, my daughter, Dottie told me about someone taking a recently deceased to the funeral home in the back of a pickup truck to avoid the expense of a hearse. I entered the bizarre idea in my computer and before I knew it, *On Ice* was written. To her goes the first acknowledgement. I would also like to thank the small but wise Seacoast Church Writers Group for their critiques and unbending support, especially Tommye Gadol for her punctuation hawk eye. Without their genuine enjoyment of excerpts, I'm not sure *On Ice* would have given me such joy to write. I also wish to acknowledge the support and encouragement from my other children, Herb, Michael, David and their spouses, and the rock of my life, my wife, Marie. Thanks also to the friends of my youth because they are the composite who is Eldridge Brewer.

Chapter One

The whole thing started one afternoon in the spring, when I was feeding the chickens. Well, not feedin''em, exactly. I had already put the feed in the troughs and refilled those thingamabobs that waters itself as the chickens drink from it. I don't know how that thing works, but when the water in the bottom where the chickens drink gets too low, the thing kind of burbles and refills the tray.

I think NASCAR came up with it for racecar drivers so they wouldn't have to make pit stops for a drink of water. It must be real hard lapping at the water, though, whilst you tryin' to drive the car six hundred miles an hour. That's probably why come they decided to use it for chickens. Daddy bought six of the watering things from Furman Freeman's Farm Fence and Fertilizer Company.

Anyway, I got to wondering if it hurt chickens when they lay eggs. Mama says it hurts real bad to have a baby, which is supposed to be kind of like laying an egg. I don't know nothing about that, but I spend so much time messing with the chickens, I wanted to know. So, I was watching a hen to see whether it hurt when she dropped an egg.

What was I gonna do if it did hurt—kiss it and make it better? I dadgum sure wasn't going to do that! Besides, there's this one rooster that would spur hell out of my butt was I to mess with his hens. I think he gets jealous because he thinks I'm a rooster like him, only taller.

Anyway, that's when it started, when I was watching a hen to see her lay an egg. She was a big red hen and she just walked around lazy-like, goin'"gaaawwwww, gaaaaw" like she was in love.

I thought that red hen was fixin' to drop a egg, as sure as a fart don't fog a window, when my little sister, Ethel, come running from the house hollering something about Tyrane Percival having a boner. That just shocked the bejeebers out of me. You know, her talking about having boners and all. I didn't know she knew about those things. She's not but nine and a half, most three years younger than me.

Mama says Ethel was a surprise, which I still ain't figured out. I mean, does she mean she surprised her being born, or does she mean she was surprised she was a girl 'stead of a boy like me? I think she meant she was surprised she wasn't a boy. She must have known she was going to be born. Big as a woman gets, she knows she's either gonna have a baby or a seed she swallowed has done growed into a great big watermelon.

I tried to watch the hen while I talked to her.

"What in the bippity-bop are you hollerin' about?" I turned and asked, but then I got real mad because, while my head was turned, it happened. There it was, a tan egg rolled across the chicken house floor, and that old red hen was walking off like she didn't know nothin' about it.

Real angry, I said, "Now look what you gone and done. She dropped her egg while you was carryin' on, and I missed it."

Ethel talks with her hands, her hips, and, well, put it like this—she waves everything. If you're not careful, she'll knock you ass over teakettle just saying good mornin'.

All a-tither, she said, "Tyrane choked on a bone, Eldridge! Aunt Bessie come runnin' to the house huffin' and puffin' and wailin' and goin' on like a crazy person. She said Tyrane was blue as a circus balloon!"

The red hen started cackling like it was the funniest thing she ever heard. The egg must not have hurt, 'cause she wouldn't of laughed about Tyrane.

I asked, "What are you talkin' about, Punky?" I call her Punky. "That's a long way for a woman big as Aunt Bessie to run. It's a flyin' wonder she didn't have a heart attack like Brother Snerkle at the Fourth of July sack races last year. How come she didn't just call Mama on the stupid phone." I said and grinned silly-like.

It made her mad 'cause she said, all haughty the way she sometimes does, "Well, how am I to know that? It ain't funny, Eldridge Brewer."

She stamped her foot so hard I thought it would go through the half-inch plywood floor of the chicken house.

"Mama's tryin' to get her calmed down and wants you to run over to her house and see to Tyrane. Aunt Bessie is goin' on so, you cain't get no sense out of her."

She grabbed my hand and started pulling hard as she could, and that's when I seen she was fixin' to cry, and I felt bad about thinking about Brother Snerkle rolling into the lake at the Fourth of July Picnic.

Brother Snerkle was a real short round fella, roly-poly, ya might say and he was leading the race. He had that sack pulled up under his armpits and bouncin' down the hill like yesterday's tomorrow going to the finish line. The lake where they got the water for whiskey stills in the old days was just to the right of the line.

All of a sudden, Brother Snerkle hollered, "Aaaaawww shiiiiiiiit." Then he disappeared into the sack which started to roll faster and faster. It veered onto the dock just haulin' boogie. The sack, with Brother Snerkle's feet stickin' out, sailed into the middle of the Moonshine Memorial Lake makin the biggest splash you ever did see.

Me and Ethel hurried to the house and I was near knocked over by what I found in our kitchen. Aunt Bessie was goin' on somethin' awful. She was at the kitchen table wiping her face and eyes with paper towels. She sometimes blew her nose and shook her head back and forth. She was a female version of Brother Snerkle only a whole lot bigger. Her face made me think of the ones in the funny papers to teach you how to draw cartoons—round with bright pink cheeks, big button nose, and circular eyes. You know what I mean, you draw circles cutting across one another, fill 'em in with a pink crayon, and bingo you've got a fat face.

"What happened, Aunt Bessie?" I asked. Bessie was married to my father's brother, Uncle Arthur.

I guess that was the wrong thing to ask, because all she did was wail and bawl. Each of her catchy sobs shook the whole house. I even heard the glasses rattle in the cupboard.

Mama was upset at Aunt Bessie for not getting a hold of herself and talking sense. To me, she said, all worried and aggravated, "I don't know what happened, Eldridge, the way she's carryin' on so. She says that Tyrane choked on a chicken bone but coughed it up. Then he was out by the chicken house and wouldn't answer when she hollered at him. It don't make no sense!"

Aunt Bessie pressed a hand to her heart and wailed, "He didn't move, Mary Elizabeth. He coughed so hard on the bone. His face turned purple as a plum ..."

She covered her face and snorted into still another towel.

Mama said, "Eldridge, Bessie's afraid something happened after all that coughing and all. She's so befuddled and goin' on so, I don't think I ought to leave her. You run over there and see about Tyrane. He's probably just fine. You know how he is when he's playing that fiddle. He don't hear nothing but what's in his head."

Bessie tried to get a grip on herself, which is kind of like somebody grabbing a blob of silly putty.

"After he coughed up the bone, he said he didn't want no more supper. He just took his fiddle outside. I called him and called ..."

Mama ripped off another paper towel from the roll by the kitchen sink and handed it to Aunt Bessie, who wadded up the one she had and added it to a huge pile in the center of the table.

Bessie went on, ending in a wail, "I tried to call y'all but I—I couldn't remember y'all's nuuuummmberrr."

I was a little spooked at first about goin' over there by myself, I'll admit. Tyrane was kind of different—you might even say strange. He'd tell jokes, but instead of laughing, everybody would just look puzzled. Mama says he was the worse storyteller she ever heard. Tyrane was Aunt

Bessie's brother. He came to live with her a few years after the big red thresher threshed Uncle Arthur.

Everybody was nice to him and all that, but Tyrane just didn't fit in. He was the only white sock in a drawer full of black ones. In a crowded room, he looked lost. In an empty room, he looked scared. Outside, he looked like he belonged inside, and inside, he looked like he wanted to find the door.

There was only one time when Tyrane was comfortable, one time when he was the one that belonged and nobody else fit, when he could command a room like a four-star general. When Tyrane Percival folded a handkerchief, nestled it under his chin and drew bow across fiddle, the world stopped to listen and to taste the memories he brought up with his music. If you didn't keep time to Tyrane's fiddle, they threw dirt on you and said "ashes to ashes." "The Orange Blossom Special" came alive in his fiddle as surely as ever a locomotive clickety-clacked on a track. With every scrape or draw of that bow, you saw puffs of smoke in time with the choo-choo, heard the creak of great big springs, and pictured the Special comin' round the mountain when she comes.

I was the fastest runner in Jupiter Bluff, but I swear I never ran harder in my life. I think I knew what I was going to find, and I dreaded it, yet it made me run all the harder. Maybe I was in a hurry to prove my fears were silly, I don't know, but all the same, I ran 'til my heart was fit to bust through my chest.

I'd guess it was about a mile to Aunt Bessie's, which sits on a kind of knoll. Like us and everybody else in Jupiter Bluff, they got a farm, probably twenty or thirty acres, and they plant most of it with corn and Crowder peas. They plant some tobacco, too, but not as much as they once did. Everywhere you turn these days somebody's carryin' on about how smoking causes cancer, pink eye, gasoline shortages, democrats and divorce, and I don't know what all else.

They got a couple of horses and a milk cow and as many chickens as we got, but they don't get as many eggs. Mama says she gives our chickens something special to make 'em lay so good. I think she means the Hadacol she gives me to put in the water thingamabob.

The house was graveyard quiet when I went through the opened gate. Old Whistler greeted me on the porch, whining and pawing at me with his long forelegs. His tail wagged back and forth, and he pushed his wet muzzle into my hand trying to get me to scratch him behind the ears. He let loose one of his namesake farts, as he always did when he was excited.

I peered through the screen door and banged on it a few times loud enough to wake a sleeping elephant, but I didn't get a answering shout. After another couple of shouts and bangs on the door, I opened it and went inside. The living room and parlor were empty and the TV was off. Aunt Bessie liked to watch TV, but Tyrane didn't. He'd go outside and play his fiddle for the chickens.

The kitchen smelled of fresh fried chicken and peas, probably cooked with some onions and ham. Man, it smelled good! Sure enough, on the counter, I found a platter of chicken legs and a wing, and on the stove, there was rice and a big pot full of Crowder peas in that goooood brown juice, all still warm.

On the table was one empty plate and another half-eaten plate of chicken and peas and a glass of tea, ice melted to a dark bottom. It appeared that Tyrane up and left the rest of his dinner on the table after he choked on the bone. Tyrane often took his dinner to the barnyard where he would toss tidbits to the chickens, maybe give Whistler a bite, and play his fiddle. Sometimes in the yard at home around dinnertime, I imagined that I could actually hear him playin' "Blue Eyes Crying in the Rain." The chokin' probably ruined his appetite so he just went out to play his fiddle.

I let my breath out in relief when I looked out the back door—I didn't know I was holding it. In the fading afternoon light, I could see the old rocking chair out by the chicken house. Tyrane sat there with his fiddle in his lap, I guessed thinking up a tune to play. His head was cocked to the side, the way he did when somebody asked him to play something special.

I started outside, but those peas smelled soooo good! Seemed like Tyrane was all right, so I got me a big plate of peas and rice and took it outside with me. Maybe he'd let me play the Special for him. I was getting pretty good at it.

Plate in hand, I pushed open the screen door and went outside, scooping peas and rice into my mouth with a spoon. Tyrane didn't turn around, but I anticipated the lopsided grin that I was sure he reserved only for me, since I was the onliest one he would let play his fiddle.

Around a mouthful of the best peas and rice I ever et, I said, "Why ain't you playin' the fiddle, Tyrane? Aunt Bessie liked to had a heart attack comin' to git me. She thought you done had a heart attack or some such …"

Tyrane Percival didn't turn around to look at me. He didn't do anything. His right hand was holding the bow, and his left still gripped the neck of his fiddle the way he did when he was fixin to notch it under his chin. He was gazing across the chicken yard kind of sad like, as if he was seeing something far off or from a long time ago.

Or something lost.

Those green eyes of his staring off across the chicken yard and not seeing anything will haunt me 'til it comes my time to go.

I reckon I cried then. I was the onliest one he would let play his fiddle.

I cried a lot.

I disremember the next couple of hours. It was just people comin' and goin'. Mama's people, mostly.

Daddy's people came around some after they took my Daddy and sent him to someplace way the hell and gone to fight some stupid war that don't nobody give a rat's ass about now. A lot of men died in that war and other wars, too, but for what I don't know. I don't think anybody knows. I read somewhere that there's still two Koreas, two Vietnams and people all over the world shootin' at one another for reasons don't none of 'em even remember.

The hell of it is they took my Daddy from me and there wasn't no damn reason for it. And my Daddy's still gone. They took him from me, damn 'em!

Anyhow, after a couple of years, we didn't see my Daddy's people much except at Christmas time or some other big do.

Uncle Felix was there in that fancy white linen suit and expensive shiny blue dressy shirt. There might have been some others from Daddy's side too, I don't know. There was a lot of people from town.

I was upstairs in my room with my arm across my eyes when Aunt Bessie come in. She sat on the edge of my bed, and I liked to have rolled off onto the floor, the mattress sagged so bad. Her face was all puffy from cryin', and her eyes was red from rubbing with paper towels and handkerchiefs.

She put a cigar box on my bed and said, "My brother wouldn't let folks get close to him. You were the only one. He said if things had been different, he might have had a boy like you his own self."

She stopped talkin' for a minute, and I knew it was real hard for her, so I didn't say nothing.

"Tyrane didn't have nothing when he come to live with me," she went on, "just the clothes on his back, that cigar box there, and his fiddle. It ain't been three days gone but what he told me that if anything ever happened to him, I was to give you his fiddle and bow."

Aunt Bessie held it up, kissed it and then laid the fiddle and bow on my stomach. I guess I stared at her like a fool with my mouth open and jaws that didn't work no more.

After a real thick moment, she said, "He told me you could be a real artist if you wanted to. He really meant it, too." She paused, and then hefted the cigar box. "I thought to go through the stuff in this here, then I thought maybe you might want to do that instead. It'll just set me to bawling again anyways."

She leaned down, patted my hand, then got up and went to the door. She filled my bedroom door as she stood there. In her pale pink dress, she looked like a great big old tent. I don't think all angels are slim, pretty little pixies; some look like big old tents.

I didn't know what to say or do, so I just stared and felt stupid. No, I felt—I felt small, maybe, not worthy, you know? I wanted to say thank you, but my mouth wouldn't work.

She almost whispered, "If Tyrane liked you that much, you gonna grow up to be somebody special, Eldridge Brewer."

Then I cried some more.

The Sheriff and the County Coroner went to Bessie's and done what sheriffs and coroners are supposed to do.

According to my friend "Peepee" Phing Phong, (I swear that is his name. Ho Chee is what his oriental folks named him, but this is America, and soon as us kids seen his last name on the blackboard at school, he was "Peepee" forever. How could we holler across a ball field, "Hey, Ho," or "Hey, Chee," or, how about, "Hey, Ping Pong, hit the ball!" People would look at us like we done gone crazy.) the Sheriff makes sure there ain't no foul play, you know, some murderer skulking about, and Peepee says that the Coroner is the one what says you're dead right enough. I don't know as I believe that about the Coroner. But, Peepee says if there wasn't nobody, some jackass would bury a poor guy that was just dead drunk. I reckoned that he had a point. Peepee was one of the smarter fellas in my class.

Before the area became a park, Moonshine Memorial Lake was where there used to be so many whiskey stills that you could get fallin' down, sloppy-ass drunk just drinking the water. That's probably why the Sheriff and Coroner liked goin' out there all the time.

Anyway, they was all day fishing together out at Moonshine Memorial Lake, so it was quite a while before they got around to looking at Tyrane. When they did, they agreed that Tyrane had—I ain't spellin' this right I don't think but—a anyoorism of the semicolon, or a coronetical thrombosis or something or other like that which I guess is fancy words for heart attack.

Until they got there, we covered him with Aunt Bessie's pink tablecloth with colorful pictures of red and yellow fruit, and what with old Whistler's barking and whistling, the chickens didn't get after Tyrane. Meanwhile, everybody gathered at our house.

Tyrane Percival's passing might have been simple had things just moved along a normal path, and if I hadn't pitched such a hissy fit. It wouldn't have got so muddy-marled up if Felton Haliday hadn't got mixed into things and if we … Well, you'll see.

Chapter Two

I poked through Tyrane's cigar box, and I could hear them downstairs arguing about something or other, but I ignored the noise and concentrated on the little box. I found a picture of The Funshiners, a group of musicians in fancy getups. One of 'em was Tyrane in a white suit. I knew he played in some bands way back when, but he never talked much about it.

I also found a stack of letters from back in the '60s addressed to Tyrane Percival, Angola Prison, Louisiana. A girl name of Leona had signed them, and she'd put kisses all over them, too.

I knew they was love letters, 'cause she started with "My love" and wrote such mushy stuff as "Oh, Ty, I miss you so much, I cry myself to sleep." I felt like the lowest scum on earth reading Tyrane's mail that way uninvited. I shook it off, though, 'cause something made me understand that I had to do it.

Voices drifted up from downstairs. I heard Mama say something about us not having any money, and I heard Uncle Felix giving Tyrane all manner of hell for not putting money back so's the rest of us wouldn't go to the poorhouse providing for his burial. He shouted right loud that "It was an un-Christian thing to do!"

Shoot! I bet he ain't saved none of the money he's snookered folks out of for them junk heaps he sells. I wonder how many folks Felix ripped off at Friendly Felix's Used Cars. I wanted to shout down the stairs: How un-Christian is that, you loudmouthed asshole? I bet if my Daddy was still around, he'd put him in his place.

But, he's not. He's not.

Another important thing I found in the box was an old yellowed newspaper clipping about a man arrested trying to rob a liquor store in Iberia Parrish, Louisiana. That man was my friend, Tyrane Percival.

Aunt Bessie's pleading voice drifted up from downstairs. "We cain't let him be buried like a pauper, y'all. He's my brother."

Even upstairs, I could hear how desperate she was about it.

Someone who might have been our neighbor on the other side said, "Jupiter Bluff has a graveyard for indigents like Tyrane, I think. That wouldn't cost so much, would it?"

Punky came in my room and tried to get me to talk to her, but I gave her a dirty look. Then I felt bad about that and explained to her, "I'm sorry, Punky. I don't feel like playin' right now, okay? Why don't you go out to the barn and check on Esmeralda."

That's our cow, who still gives milk, but Mama allows how it ain't gonna be long 'fore she dries up, and we have to eat her.

I was surprised at how meekly Punky nodded. She just surrendered which wasn't like her. She sniffled and said simply, "All … all right, Eldy," and closed the door. Eldy was her name for me when things was warm and fuzzy. She used it when she was hurtin', too.

Damn, Eldridge Brewer, you can be so stupid. I called her back, got up and give her a big hug.

"It's all right, Punky," I assured her. "Don't cry, heah."

She was upset about Tyrane, too, and needed a hug from her big brother. I held her a minute and wiped a tear away with my thumb. She smiled at me, and a moment later, I heard her skipping down the stairs almost the way she always does.

I might have stopped rummaging in the box, but something made me keep on looking. It felt weird poking into what was left of a man with a fiddle who was my friend … maybe more than that really. Then I found the third thing.

It was another newspaper clipping tore out real ragged, no more than two inches long. It was about a woman named Leona LeSeur, aged twenty-four, who had died of cancer, it said, and was to be buried the next day in Shady Rest Cemetery in New Iberia, Louisiana. I stared at the shabby little cigar box and the story it told. I ain't never felt that way about nothing before nor since. All these years, I wondered why Tyrane seemed to be looking back, like there was something behind him that he couldn't have.

What it was that Tyrane couldn't have was Leona LeSeur.

The living room of our house was wall-to-wall people—relatives, neighbors and a bearded fella in a funny hat looking a little out of place. Everybody was listening to an argument involving Aunt Bessie, Mama, Uncle Felix Plunkett, and George Carsewell, our neighbor on the opposite side from Aunt Bessie, and several others who was friends of both families.

In Jupiter Bluff, nobody had much money. Wait a minute, that ain't right. Nobody had no money—any money, I mean. My teacher, Miss Fanny Hurlbutte, was always fussin' at me about twice negatives. Uncle Felix was raisin' hell about the cost of planting Tyrane and was getting a lot of support from the others for a pauper's burial.

Several folks offered to chip in, but the cost was still out of sight, mainly on account of a cemetery plot. Daddy once told me that the Indians used to put dead people in trees and let the birds have 'em. He said it wasn't like you're layin' there watching a buzzard pecking your eyes out. But, I guess that wasn't a Christian way to dispose of dead folks.

Looking as unhappy about it as she did, Mama said to Aunt Bessie, "Bessie, honey, what else can we do? Nobody's got no money to do no better. Don't nobody want it this way." As convincing and sympathetic as possible, she added, "It'll be a nice send off 'cause everybody can come, and we'll get Brother Cadminster to say words over him."

Aunt Bessie was sitting on the couch in our living room with a pile of wadded damp paper towels on the coffee table at least as big as the one she had built in the kitchen earlier. There ain't no telling how many rolls of them towels she'd been through.

She dabbed at her eyes and pleaded with everyone in the room as she scanned the faces watching her. "Y'all can't let this happen to poor Tyrane! He played his fiddle for y'all every time anybody asked him to. Felix, he played it at your house when your son Oswald signed his Letter of Intent to play football for Jupiter Bluff College of Taxidermy and Auto Mechanics. Tyrane didn't have nothing to do with the school going belly up. It was them environmentalists marchin' around the Dean's house with signs callin' him a deer killer."

Uncle Felix turned away and ate a little more of that turd he had stuck in his mouth. I know they're cigars, but if it looks like a turd and smells like a turd, that might as well be a turd stuck in his mouth.

"And how about you, Matilda?" Aunt Bessie was saying. "He filled in for your husband at the high school dance 'cause your husband turned gay and run off with the shop teacher. He had blisters on his hand for a week from that gig."

Someone muttered, "So did the shop teacher."

Then she said, "Buster, Tyrane played fiddle at your place for every barbecue shindig you ever had, didn't he?"

Buster Brickflicker was standing near one of the windows drinking from a pint fruit jar, and I'm sure as shootin' sure it wasn't no tea in it. He hung his head and turned away, as if he didn't know what Aunt Bessie was talking about.

My Uncle Felix Plunkett apparently decided he was the onliest one with good sense, 'cause he started actin' like his poop don't stink.

Haughty as all get out and around his nasty cigar, he announced,

"Well, we can't set around here all day deebatin' what a fine, free fiddle Tyrane played. The old man is gone and that's the whole of it. I'll go in yonder and call Harold's Funeral Chapel, Vinyl Siding and Windows Company and tell 'em to fix him up cheap as they can. We'll plant him tomorrow at the paupers' field on Bohicketty Road, probably about two or three o'clock. You can't miss it 'cause there's a little sign, saying something about property of Jupiter Bluff, or something like that and there's a telephone number." Then he asked, "That suit everybody?"

There were some sadly murmured "yeses," but mostly, heads nodded silently, including Mama's and all of my blood kin. The stranger in the funny hat was quiet but his eyes sparkled with interest. Aunt Bessie sat on the couch quietly sniffling and dabbing. I felt awful for her, especially after what she done for me.

"No sir, that don't suit worth a flyin' frog!"

It was a young voice, a boy's angry voice, that rang out in that room. You could've heard a flea sneeze it got so quiet. For a second I didn't realize that it was my own voice.

"We gotta take him to Louisiana. We can't bury Tyrane here in no rotten city field like he wasn't nothing," I said. "We can't. It ain't right, y'all." I was holding back tears as hard as I ever in my life done. I ain't gonna cry, I kept telling myself.

Uncle Felix stared at me as if to say who the hell are you. Then he turned to Mama acting like she just farted during Reverend Cadminster's prayer. Course that happened a lot 'cause he prayed so long you might hear brrrrrppppp three or four times. Folks just couldn't help it.

Uncle Felix shook his finger at Mama and said, "Mary Elizabeth, what in hell are the children doin' in here whilst we talking about buryin' a dead man? For God's sake, you need to take the children out of here. This is not something for brats to get mixed up in."

'Fore Mama could answer, I hollered at my uncle, "You shut up! You just shut the hell up, you asshole! He was my friend, too. He gave me his fiddle and was teachin' me to play it. You ain't gonna throw him away like trash. He belongs in Louisiana. He ain't trash!"

I stomped my foot and threw the ham sandwich I had been eating at Uncle Felix.

I slop sandwiches pretty good with Mama's homemade mayonnaise, so the bread splatted on each side of his white linen blazer and started slowly smearing its way down. A slab of ham plopped against his eyeglasses and hung there while a string of ham fat twirled around the frame near his ear.

I seen all this through a torrent of tears, and I was sobbing so hard my mouth couldn't make the words that I was thinking.

Mama was stunned at what I done, which I knew was awful, but I couldn't help it. I couldn't let them bury Tyrane that way. Between catches of breath, I managed to say, "He had (sob) a girlfriend (sob). She died (sob) when he (sob) was in (sob) prison. She had blue eyes."

Uncle Felix was mad enough to spit nails. When he snatched off his glasses, slimy with grease and mayonnaise, they went flying across the room with a string of ham fat spinning like a tiny whirly-gig. He took the sloppy pieces of bread, one in each hand, held by two fingers each, and whilst wrinkling his nose, looked for some place to deposit the drippy things.

He yelled at my mama, "My God, look what that boy has done! He has ruined my jacket. Mary Elizabeth, that boy needs a sound thrashing. If you don't see to it, I shall do it myself!"

Since he couldn't find a better place, he put the bread in a nearby glass that was half full of ice, and then held his hands up, unsure about what to do with them next.

"Please get him out of here until we have finished with this funeral business. Tyrane was all right, but there's no damn reason for all this folderol. The man is dead, for Christ's sake. Look at me, I'm a mess."

Mama put her arms around me as much to protect me from Uncle

Felix, I think, as to console me. She began trying to lead me out of the living room.

"Come on, Eldy. I know how much you loved Tyrane. Nobody was talking disrespectful of him. It's just a matter of not having the money. We'll have a nice service for him, I promise. Okay?"

I pulled back from her and pleaded. "Mama, you don't understand. Listen to me! Tyrane went to jail when he was in Louisiana. He was in love with a woman there and she died. That's why he was sad all the time. We have to take him to Louisiana and bury him next to her."

Uncle Felix shooed one of my cousins from a chair, sat down and tried to clean the smear of mayonnaise off his jacket, which he had taken off. Without the jacket, you could see that fancy fine sky-blue dress shirt he wore so proudly wasn't so fine after all. Holes big as a cantaloupe was worn through both sleeves at the elbows and there was a tear under one arm. Somehow, the asshole had gotten mayonnaise on the end of his cigar, too, so now you could smell burning eggs in the room.

"For God's sake, don't mollycoddle the child, Mary Elizabeth. He needs a good beating." Snapped Felix, angrier yet that his efforts worsened the smears.

Aunt Bessie got up off the couch, which took considerable effort. She said firmly, "You leave him alone, Felix Plunkett. Eldridge is upset. He was very close to Tyrane. This has hit him real hard, and you talking like his friend don't matter none was just too much for him."

"Upset. Upset, hell! He's just a spoiled brat," snorted Uncle Asshole.

A loud new voice pierced the room like a spear.

"That boy is upset right enough, but it would do you well to listen, on account he's tryin' to tell y'all something important."

The voice was deep and scratchy, the kind that snakes its way betwixt, between and above other voices in a crowded room. It belonged to the bearded man and had something in it to make you shut up and listen. For the second time the room went quiet.

Our neighbor, George Carsewell, looked the stranger up and down suspiciously and asked, "Who might you be, mister?"

It surprised me, him asking, 'cause he hadn't offered nothing in the way of help in the cost of Tyrane's funeral except his big mouth.

Mr. Carsewell didn't even try to hide his distrust of the stranger. "What's your business here today on the occasion of the passing of one of our own?"

"Name's Felton Haliday. I am a friend—was a friend—of Tyrane Percival. I was on my way east and thought to stop off and see him. Hope y'all don't mind that I got sort of caught up in everything. Finding him passed over the river was quite a blow to me. I didn't mean to mix in where I ain't got no business, you understand, but I couldn't help but make the observation about what the boy was saying."

He hesitated for a moment in which he looked out of the window nearby and seemed to see something away off.

He continued, "The boy said something about a woman and Louisiana and prison, too. Might be that I know what he's talkin' 'bout. Was her name Leona, boy?"

His sudden mixing into things made me compose myself by the time he asked me. "Yes, sir. It was Leona LeSeur," I said, my voice kind of shaky.

I ain't ever seen this man, and Tyrane never talked about anybody all the times we was together. I was a little scared I might get Tyrane in trouble even though he had —what this fella said—crossed over the river. I went on although I was uncertain about him.

"She died, sir. I think when Tyrane was in prison at Angola in Louisiana. I – I think she had blue eyes."

Haliday smiled at me. He understood what was going on with me, I was sure of it. 'Course I didn't know myself. There was something about his smile that made me think that everything was going to be all right. He nodded slowly.

"Blue eyes? Yes, boy, about the bluest you ever did see."

Uncle Felix seemed to have calmed down a bit, and I tried not to grin at the glob of mayonnaise and piece of ham in his hair as he said testily, "Look here, Mister, what's this all about? We've got to get on with this, Hollomay, or whatever the hell your name is. The man's body is still in the yard for Christ's sake. You and the boy can go outside and reminisce about a fiddlin' jailbird and blue-eyed women if you want to, but we've got things to do here."

"He ain't no jailbird, you fat asshole!"

I turned to Mama and pleaded, "Mama, we've got to take him to Louisiana and bury him next to Leona LeSeur. Please Mama, can't we? It's only right, Mama."

I was still just a boy, you know, and I could be kind of cute, even cuddly if I had to, and I used that talent as best I could, but it wasn't near enough.

Mama said apologetically, "Eldy, a funeral is terribly expensive and among all of us, we just have enough for the basics, and that don't include a cemetery plot, which costs a pile of money."

She held me to ease the pain of what she was saying and went on, "I know how you feel, son. He was special to you, and it's hard to say goodbye. But you have to be a big boy like you were when we lost Daddy."

That last was like a knife in my gut, sharp, deep and painful. I never cried about losing Daddy. I swore I never would, 'cause I didn't lose Daddy. He was stolen from me when God wasn't lookin'!

I jerked away from her and snapped bitterly, "It ain't the same! Daddy was took from me!"

Everybody seemed to find something to look at besides me and mama. Somebody coughed. I could see they was all embarrassed. I made myself calm down and said, "He has a cemetery plot in Louisiana, Mama. See, that's what this is."

I handed her the last letter I had found in the cigar box. I dried my eyes with my shirtsleeve.

"It was not opened, Mama. I don't think Tyrane ever read it."

Mama looked at the stuff with wonder and then at Aunt Bessie and the rest of the people in the living room. When she unfolded the yellowed paper, the room was so quiet you could hear how brittle the paper was, 'cause it crinkled. After a few seconds, Mama began to read.

Dear Tyrane,

It's been a long time since you have heard from us in Louisiana. I know it's too late to tell you, but I was wrong to blame you for everything that happened. If I hadn't been such a pigheaded fool, her last few months might have been a whole lot happier with you by her side.

The doctors have told me that my time is getting short now, too. It's little consolation that an old fool wants to right a wrong that can't be righted in order to have a chance at a place in heaven. Nevertheless, I have to do what's right even at this late date and even if it's too late to get it in my record of service to the Lord.

The LeSeur family graveyard has three more spaces. One of them is where I will soon lie beside Leona's blessed Mama. The second is for Leona's brother. It would pleasure me more than I can express if you would consent to lie in the third one. It is next to Leona.

I pray that your life has been without the torment that has haunted mine over the way I treated you, that you found a love and raised a nice family. If you don't wish to use the grave plot, I can understand. However, in that event, I intend that it never be used, since it wouldn't be right that anyone but you lie beside her.

I don't deserve your forgiveness, but I beg it of you just the same.
Yours sincerely,
Edwin LeSeur.

Chapter Three

I heard an occasional shuffle of feet, Aunt Bessie sniffled softly and ice tinkled in someone's iced tea glass. I felt a little hand slip into my fingers, and I looked down at Punky. She smiled up at me, trying to take the pain out of my heart.

Somebody said, "Well I'll be damned."

"I'll take him to Louisiana by myself if I have to, Mama," I said determinedly, not thinking at all how stupid that sounded coming from me, only twelve years old and all. In my mind, I was old enough to do it. But in reality I knew I couldn't.

Uncle Felix finally broke the silence and said, "Well, that don't change things none. How in hell would we get him to New Iberia in way the hell and gone Louisiana? We can't afford that no more'n we can a damn burial plot!" He snorted and waved his arm.

There was still a blob of mayonnaise in his hair, but I couldn't laugh at it. All I could think of was Tyrane buried in a field marked only as property of Jupiter Bluff and a damn phone number.

"It wouldn't cost that much to take him down there," said Felton Haliday around a chaw of tobacco from a chunk about the size of a deck of cards. He pushed himself from the wall and stared hard at Uncle Felix with ice-cold eyes.

"Yeah, well, whose gonna do that?" asked Uncle Felix, acting like a smart ass. "Can't none of us go driving across America to put a dead man beside a girl who died twenty years ago. A jailbird at that, it now seems. None of us would be that stupid, I can tell you."

He grinned at everybody and laughed mockingly.

Haliday said, "Well, I reckon I'm the stupid one then, because I'd be honored to do it." He turned to me and added, "Me and the boy here will take him to Louisiana in my truck and bury him beside Leona LeSeur, where I think he would like to lie. That is, of course, if his Mama will allow the boy to travel with a man she ain't never seen before."

When he looked at Mama, I knew she was gonna say, "Yes," and, bless a flying monkey, I think he did too.

Felton hesitated a second, then said not meanly, "The rest of you can go straight to hell, excluding some, (grinning at Mama and Aunt Bessie) and specifically including others."

His eyes lit on Felix, and my uncle got squirmy, looking away and poking at his ear. This stranger didn't look like somebody he could buffalo.

Mama said, "Uncle Felix, I appreciate you coming today, I really do. Your concern and your advice and all, I surely do thank you for, but I think Bessie and me can work this out with Mister, uh …"

The stranger said firmly and very clearly, "Haliday, Mrs. Brewer, Felton Haliday from Minnesota, and I'm real honored to meet you good people."

He had the sharpest eyes I ever in my life saw. They was green as a magnolia leaf, and I swear to you he couldn't lie 'cause they'd give him away.

Right then I knew I was gonna like this fella. Never mind that I wondered who he was, really. Why would a fella all the way from Minnesota, which is on the other side of the whole world, come thousands of miles to Jupiter Bluff in West Virginia and want to drive another hundred thousand miles to Louisiana?

Felix Plunkett still sat wiping his jacket, getting madder again, 'cause each time he wiped at it, the smear spread worse. Somebody had plucked the ham from his hair and put it in the glass on a side table with the rest.

Ignoring her invitation to leave, he glared at Mama and said, "Dear

God, Mary Elizabeth, surely you're not going to let Eldridge go off with this—this—consorter with jailbirds! That would be irresponsible. I forbid it. The child is barely more than a tyke, he is my nephew, and I feel responsible for his safety. I'm sure if my late brother-in-law were here, he would agree."

I started to blurt the best insult I could think of, but suddenly two of Mama's fingers were pressed against my lips.

Mama blinked back angry tears, and cold as an ice tray from our fridge, she said real firm, "He's not here, Felix. He hasn't been here for a very long time. I miss him a hell of a lot, too."

She stepped away from me and faced my uncle square.

"In all these years, you haven't offered even a little pinky to help us. The only time we see you is on occasions like this or when you seem to want to show off or something. It's a little late for you to start acting like a loving uncle now. I think I'm more than able to know what's best for Eld—"

"Well!" Snapped Uncle Felix, madder now than when I hit him with the sandwich. "Maybe you better take a look at what that brat did to my suit. Look at this! Just look! Is that a proper way to raise my nephew? I think not! I will not leave until the child is dealt with."

A titter of laughter seemed to roll through the room when Mama did something I never thought she'd do.

She said, "Actually, Felix, I was just about to do that very thing."

She rummaged in the pocket of her apron and pulled out a dollar.

"Eldy, here is a reward for a fine throw of a ham sandwich. It was a perfect strike!"

Having worked his way around to be near my uncle, Felton Haliday chuckled, bent down to Felix's ear and whispered something. I don't know what it was, but my uncle's face turned white as a flying swan, and his mouth dropped open.

Uncle Felix apparently decided he wanted to be someplace else—

any place else—in a hurry, 'cause he got up and headed for the door. He jerked it open, but before he stepped out, he shot a evil look at Felton Haliday that made me shudder. As he left, Felton Haliday handed him his greasy glasses which he had retrieved from the floor.

While people ate potluck food somebody had brought in, mostly fried chicken, Mama gathered Mr. Haliday and me in the kitchen. Punky snuck in through the back door and sidled to the kitchen counter, trying to be invisible. Mama's worried look made me think I was too quick on the draw when I thought she was gonna okay me going with this stranger all the way to Louisiana.

She started out sounding like she hired him to rake the yard, you know what I mean? These here are the rules for rakin' pine straw, Mr. Haliday.

She really said, "Mr. Haliday, my name is Mary Elizabeth Brewer. This is my son, Eldridge." She hesitated when she noticed Punky there, too. "And this," she tousled Punky's blond curly hair, "is Ethel. I—"

"My name is Ethel, but you can call me Punky if you want to. My friends call me Punky," interrupted my little sister importantly.

Felton looked down at her and gave her a big, friendly grin.

"Well, I sure do want to be your friend, so I reckon I better call you Punky. Is that all right?"

Punky twisted shyly and held on to Mama's apron. From behind it, she nodded happily and said kind of grown up, "Yes, that will be fine."

It was about then that I noticed a look in my Mama's eyes that I hadn't seen in years. They purely sparkled like some of my brightest agates. What in the bibbity bop was goin' on here, I wondered?

I could tell she was trying to be an official Mama, but the sparkle didn't go away, and her smile came, went, and came back again. She spoke very firmly.

"Mr. Haliday, I will admit that I'm concerned about Eldridge going with you. No offense, but we really don't know you."

Felton stepped to the screen door, cracked it open and spat through it. He turned back to Mama and said, "No Ma'am, you don't. My friends call me Felton like friends call this cute little pixie Punky. It would please me more'n I can express if you and this boy was to be my friends. There ain't time for y'all to get to know me, if we gonna take Tyrane to the woman he loved, which I personally believe is my Christian duty. I think the boy feels that way, too. All I can tell you, Mrs. Brewer, is I ain't a bad man, and I'll look after Eldridge here like he was my own seed."

Mama's face reddened like I ain't never seen it and, I swear, her eyes sparkled even more.

Later, after I had gone to bed, I could hear voices downstairs and thought at first it was Mama and Aunt Bessie. Then curiosity got the best of me, and I crept to the head of the stairs. I couldn't see nobody, so I snuck about halfway down and craned my neck to see the front. There wasn't nobody there, but through the kitchen I could see sitting on the back steps the outline of Mama and Felton Haliday. I watched for a few minutes and heard Mama laugh like she used to when she and Daddy sat together on them steps.

It felt good to hear. It was along about then that I began thinking about Mama and Felton in the same breath. You know, maybe bein' friends and all—maybe more 'n friends.

Well …

So that's how come it was that me and Felton Haliday found ourselves on what he said was the Cold War Highway. Felton said President Eisenhower had the highways built so if Russian hordes attacked us, we'd have enough roads to get away, or if somebody dropped a atom bomb, we could haul butt on super highways. Eisenhower ought to know what he was talking about, him being a war hero and all.

We put Tyrane in one of them round plastic kiddy pools and packed around him twelve bags of ice from the 7-Eleven on Cadwallader Street, so's he'd keep 'til we got to New Iberia. The kiddy pool was really cheerful with brightly colored little cartoon fish, turtles and crabs and stuff like that all over it. It made Tyrane look like he was swimming in a fish tank with happy sea creatures dancing around him.

Actually, we had a fourth passenger. See, there was Tyrane and me, and Felton made three, and Whistler was four. He jumped into the back of Felton's restored Studebaker pickup truck when we was leaving, and we didn't know he was back there for nigh on a hundred miles.

Poor Felton liked to have wrecked the truck when we discovered Whistler. We was passing a tractor trailer, driving along pretty good, Felton telling stories about him and Tyrane and that band in the picture I found in the cigar box, The Funshiners. He was telling me that they played "gigs" all over the South when all of a sudden Whistler stuck his shaggy head in the sliding glass window and gave Felton a gawdawful sloppy-ass lick up side the face.

He hollered so loud, I thought he was kilt, and then he swerved the truck so hard it's a flyin' wonder it didn't flip over.

The melting ice sloshed all over the truck bed. I don't know how he got the truck under control, but thank a flying angel he did.

We pulled off on the shoulder to make sure we hadn't dumped Tyrane out of the kiddy pool or done something else bad in all that swerving. Whistler was just tickled to death to be with us. He whistle-farted almost steady in his excitement, and he hopped up and down in the kiddy pool, nearly drowning me and Felton.

Felton wrinkled his nose, waved his hand in front of his face and hollered, "What is that noise he's making? He stinks like … Is he farting, Eldy?"

I couldn't contain myself, I was so glad to see the big old shaggy thing.

I said, "Yes sir, Mr. Haliday. That's why come his name is Whistler. Ain't it boy?"

I fondled that big old wet head, and Whistler's tail thumped on the truck bed like a trip-hammer.

I didn't know what kind of dog Whistler was. Tyrane said a fella give him Whistler when he was a pup. He said it was 'cause he was grateful for him playing the fiddle at his wife's funeral. How about that for a good swap? I wonder what he would have give him for playing at their wedding, a skunk?

Whistler was a big reddish-yellow dog with long, shaggy hair. Peepee says you could mop the gym at my school with his sweeping tail. He had big brown eyes that could smile or cry, like a person. Tyrane said he was a Heinz dog, 57 varieties, and then he laughed. I didn't understand that joke, but I laughed, too.

You did have to get used to Whistler. I mean, when he whistled, it could peel the paint off a garage. You just had to make sure you weren't downwind.

We got back underway after rearranging Tyrane in the kiddy pool and putting all the ice that was thrown out back into it.

We would have to drive for two days, Felton said. Aunt Bessie had used one of my crayons to draw the route from Jupiter Bluff, West Virginia, to New Iberia, Louisiana, on two different maps. I gotta say I didn't know it was that far. We were going through Virginia, Tennessee, Alabama, and I don't know how many other states.

I reckon I kept up a pretty steady chatter, with Felton Haliday nodding sometimes or glancing at me and saying, "uh huh." To tell the truth, I don't think he was paying a lot of attention, so I ran out of stuff to talk about and got pretty quiet myself.

The windshield wipers kept time in a patch of rain we went through, and I prodded Felton until he talked more about Tyrane and the band. They were part of a "shit-kicker band," he called it. I took that to mean they didn't play city music where everybody's goin'"doowaaa, doowaa" or "boogidy boogidy."

Trucks created clouds of spray, but it didn't seem to bother Felton as he talked about it, "We called ourselves The Funshiners. Tyrane Percival and The Funshiners. We played all over, Louisiana, the Carolinas, Mississippi, all over the South. We did Nashville, too. We were gonna do the Grand Ole Opry, but Tyrane nixed that in no uncertain terms.

"We had a young black fella played bass, name of Skyler Boudreaux. He was pretty good, too. We were all set to do the Opry the next Saturday night show when the Opry talent manager told Tyrane, 'We got y'all a good bass man too.' Tyrane allowed as how we already had a good bass man. The fella said, 'Yeah, but he's a nigger, and you can't use a black man in Rhymer Auditorium.'"

Felton continued, "Back then performing on the Grand Ole Opry was a ticket to the big time, but that didn't matter to Tyrane. He cussed that fella for a sombitch, grabbed him by the neck of his jacket and the seat of his pants and threw him out of the bar. The last we saw of the Grand Ole Opry was its talent manager splashing in a mud puddle in the parking lot of the Silver Dollar Bar in Memphis. I 'member it like it was yesterday. As that fella sailed headlong out the door, Tyrane hollered at him that if Skyler Boudreaux couldn't play Rhymer, he could stick the Grand Ole Opry up his butt."

Felton settled back in his seat a bit and said, "We had a time all right. We surely did."

"Why'd y'all quit then, Mr. Haliday?" I asked.

We were coming up on a tractor-trailer, while yet another, a big red one, was passing us. Before Felton could answer me, the truck crowded us and Felton had to swerve onto the shoulder. He laid a cussin' on the trucker, and sped up until he was just ahead of it. Felton leaned out the window and then spewed a glorious stream of brown juice at least five feet straight up in the air.

He hollered at me over the roar of the truck, "That ought to slow that big sucker down some. Them trucks is a roarin' ass nuisance!"

Felton grinned at me and added happily, "Tobacco juice can make a helluva mess, and it's hard to get off, too."

I turned around to watch, and I could see the trucker rocking back and forth in his seat trying to look around a huge blob of what looked like smeared crap on the truck's windshield. He slowed down, and then I saw him pull to the shoulder and stop. A group of motorcycles slowed down, too, and they might have stopped, but I wasn't sure about that.

Felton went quiet. I waited for him to answer my question. Finally, I said, "Well?"

"Well what?"

"Why'd y'all quit?"

The people in a convertible going by us were craning their necks at the old Studebaker, or maybe they were looking at Whistler. Whatever it was, they had admiring expressions on their faces. As they went by, Felton nodded at 'em and gave them a wave.

I stared at him hard until he answered my question.

"Tyrane fell in love is why we quit, boy. When he seen Leona's blue eyes in the rain at that Cajun picnic in New Iberia, his eyes watered, his tongue stuck to the roof of his mouth, and his heart was hers forever."

"How come that made y'all stop, Mr. Haliday? Leona LeSeur didn't like Tyrane's music?"

He cut his eyes at me with a smirky grin that I noticed he used a lot. He said, "Look here, boy. If we gonna be riding together for two days with a dead man floatin' around in a kiddy pool in the truck and a dog whistle-fartin' across Dixie, can't you call me Felton?"

"Yes sir." I tried it out. "Felton, yes sir!"

"It certainly wasn't nothin' like that. God, she loved his music. When he played that fiddle for her, it made the sweetest sound you ever in your life heard. No, it was her folks. Her Daddy pitched the biggest fit ever I seen a grown man do. He made Tyrane and Leona miserable. They had to sneak around like weasels. It was a shame, too, because they had the cleanest, purest love I think two folks could have."

Felton didn't say anything more for a couple of seconds. I think he was remembering.

The truck's tires beat out a rhythm on the cracks in the pavement. They went "thrup, thrup, thrup." The sound filled the truck's little cab, while Felton's face got the saddest expression I ever saw.

Then, a baldheaded fella wearing holey jeans, a leather jacket without a shirt, and snakeskin boots drew up alongside us on his motorcycle. He gave Felton Haliday a closer look than was normal, it seemed to me, but I thought no more about it.

Along about two o'clock in the afternoon, Felton asked me, "You gettin' hungry, Eldy? We still got a long ways to go before we stop to spend the night and get a sit-down meal. I figure to do that near Chattanoogy."

We had bought us some Dr. Pepper, cheese crackers, you know, Nabs, and crap like that when we bought gas for the truck. I like them little chocolate moon pies and Whistler liked them too, so I got a couple of those. We put the drinks in the ice of the kiddy pool with Tyrane, so they got good and cold.

"Yes, sir, I could eat something, I guess. Mama fixed us a "care package" she called it. I seen her wrap some fried chicken and make some baloney sandwiches, too."

"There's a rest stop comin' up, probably. We'll pull off, take a leak and stretch our legs and eat something."

He glanced out the sliding glass window into the back and added, "Whistler probably needs a rest, too. There's a length of rope back there somewhere you can use for a leash. We don't want him to go wandering around providing aromatic music to everybody's picnic."

We pulled off at the bright blue rest area sign. After we ate, I went to the area where there was a sign saying you could walk your dog. I guess that was so they wouldn't leave piles of dog pookey where everybody was picnicking. Felton was putting our lunch leavings in a paper sack behind the seat, when I noticed an old man standing there looking at the Studebaker.

He said to Felton, "That old truck brings back some memories, friend. She sure is handsome. Did you restore her yer own self?"

The old guy looked as old as the crossing guard at my school that Peepee says is near on to a hundred. Peepee has a way of knowing these things on account he's a oriental. They have mystic powers, ya know, like that weird woman at the carnival every year.

Haliday looked out from under the brim of that funny looking little hat he wore that looked like a upside down bowl and answered, "Well, ya might, in a manner of speakin', say I did, but that wouldn't be altogether accurate."

Felton let his gaze flow from one end of the old pickup to the other.

"You tellin' me you bought her in that condition? Somebody spent a lot of time restoring her to make her look that good. Must've cost you a pretty penny," the man said as he started a slow, admiring walk around the truck's bed.

Felton Haliday had a slow way of talking, kind of like molasses poured from a boot. He chuckled.

"Well, she did and then again, she didn't. I bought her new in 1959 and treated her like a delicate princess. When she scraped her knee, I kissed it to make it well and made her take proper medicine when she was sick. Give her a new paint job for a new dress when she needed it, and she appreciated my kindness. If that means it cost me a pretty penny, then it did right enough, but I never regretted a dime of it, thank you very much."

The old man stared at Felton, nodded admiringly and strolled off with several looks back at the pea green truck.

"She sure is pretty, Mister," he said.

The next encounter we had at the rest stop wasn't so warm and fuzzy.

Just as I got in the truck and settled in, I glanced at the entrance lane to the rest stop and saw a red tractor-trailer suddenly veer toward the car parking area. Several motorcycles followed it. It didn't mean nothing at first, other than I thought it was curious, you know a big ole truck like that ignoring the signs and all.

Then I 'most filled my britches. I punched Felton on the shoulder and said scaredy-like, "Oh Lord, Felton. Ain't that the truck we—?"

Felton ain't batted an eye, and didn't push on the floor starter neither.

"Yeah, I believe it is," he said.

He bit off a chunk of tobacco, grinned at me and added, "I better make sure my weapon is loaded," and he sat there chewing, waiting.

The big truck came to a halt behind the Studebaker with a scraping of brakes and a hiss like a thousand librarians shushin' the reading room. Whilst it was rocking, the driver, a huge guy in jeans, clambered down out of the cab mad enough to kill. The sleeves of his checkered shirt were rolled up on arms like tree trunks. He cussed and went on about catching the bastard that threw a bag of pookey on his truck.

Felton chewed that tobacco the way a happy cow chews straw and grinned at me as if he brought me to see the circus, like to say, "Looky yonder, Eldy, ain't this fun watching the elephants?"

My heart was beating like the Jack of Spades in a bicycle wheel.

The big man marched up to Felton's side of the pickup and roared at him to roll down the window. His face was red and puffed up.

So mad his esses sprayed the window with spit, he blustered, "Get out of that truck, you wise ass sombitch!"

He put huge hands on the top of the cab and rocked it so hard I could hear the ice slosh out of the pool onto the metal truck bed.

Whistler was trying to get at the man, snarling like to kill him. Above it all, I told Felton later that I thought I heard the loudest whistle he ever turned loose.

Felton was still grinning and seemed to be getting a kick out of the whole thing. When the guy drew back his fist to break the glass, Felton rolled it down, leaned out just a little, and I seen his head jerk in a sort of tossing motion. A big, long, thick strip of brown sludge spewed across the space between Felton and the truck driver, hitting him full in the face. The man's nose cleaved the tobacco juice into nearly perfect halves, one into the left eye the other into the right.

The truck driver staggered away clawing at his eyes and cussing like yesterday's tomorrow. His foot caught on a crack in the pavement and he fell on his fat ass. Along about then, Whistler give up trying to get at him from the truck bed and jumped out snarling, barking and with eyes like an attacking wolf.

That's when I started to think of the truck driver as a poor man, not in wealth or nothing, but in luck. The man landed with his legs wide apart, and Whistler went for the best grip he thought he could get. When old Whistler clamped down on that fella's crotch, I never heard a man holler so loud in my life, before nor since.

Moving as if he had all day, Felton got out, caught a hold of Whistler's rope leash and pulled him off. While the man hollered that he couldn't see and held his hands cupped over his privates, Felton stood over him and said, "I can't stand rude behavior, Mister. Just 'cause your truck is bigger 'n mine, don't mean you can run me off the road. If you had let it go the way we left ya, you wouldn't be wriggling around on the ground holding your balls."

Several people came over to see what the ruckus was all about. They gathered round the truck driver who was holding onto his crotch goin' "aaaaarrrrrggghhhh," while a group of motorcyclists watched from a ways off. For a minute, I could have sworn one of them was the baldheaded guy I saw earlier.

A young blonde girl said to the skinny fella she was with, "I think he's the driver what cut you off back there, Jimmy."

"Yeah, I think it is, but he sure as hell looks like he ain't gonna hog any more roads for a while." Her skinny partner nodded.

"And I believe the ladies at the truck stops are in for a big disappointment, too," he added with a satisfied smirk,

Chapter Four

We climbed back into the Studebaker and left the rest area. Felton started whistling, as if damn near blinding a mean-eyed truck driver was all in a day's work.

It was still right warm with the sun on the backside of the day. We drove under a beautiful blue sky. I know we were taking my friend to his burial, but somehow I felt good—not as good as when Mama comes in my room and snugs the cover under my chin not knowing I ain't really asleep, but good.

A little while later Felton said, "I noticed the ice is meltin' away right fast. I reckon we're gonna have to buy some more soon. If we don't, Tyrane is gonna develop a pretty strong case of B.O."

He glanced at his watch. "We ought to be in Chattanoogy by seven or eight o'clock, and we can get a full sit-down meal. Then I want to find us a place to sleep. There was a time when I could drive straight through, but I ain't up to them long hauls no more. My ass starts to think there's a car seat growin' on it."

"You talking like we cain't get us a room, Felton. Why not? Don't we have enough money?"

"Money's not the problem, Eldy." He gave me an odd look and thumbed at the truck bed. "What the blue blazes we gonna do with Fart Blossom back there? We can't tie him up in the truck, he'll howl his dadgum head off. I know he's almost like a dog of your'n, but I don't relish sleepin' with him whistlin' his contentment all night in a stuffy motel room. I don't like it none, but we're gonna have to drop him off at one of them dog shelters. We can't drive all night."

Everything had been going so good since I pitched my fit at the house, and Felton Haliday turned out to be so nice and all, that this hit me like a thrown sack of pookey. He was right, of course. Whistler was not a housedog. Lord, let me tell you, Whistler was not a housedog!

My heart sank like a bobber with a lead too heavy. In the hours since Tyrane crossed over, I had got to thinking of Whistler as my own dog, just like Tyrane's fiddle.

Talking fast, begging really, I said, "He won't be no trouble, Felton. I'll see after him. I promise he won't whistle in the room. He don't whistle when he's calm. It'll be all right. Tyrane let him in the house all the time. He was extra careful not to get him excited. We don't have to leave him. We don't, okay?"

Felton shook his head, unhappy, but I thought his mind was made up when he said, "Eldy, when he does his thing, damn if it ain't the gawdawfullest stink I ever smelt. We can't keep him in the room. Motels won't let you have a pet, and it's fer damn sure they ain't gonna let a dog like Whistler in their rooms."

He stuck his head out the window and spat.

I pleaded, "We can sneak him in, Felton! I'm good at stuff like that. Me 'n Peepee sneak stuff in class and in the gym all the time. We ain't never been caught neither. I can do it, Felton. Please, sir, don't take Whistler to the pound."

I could feel I was going to cry, and I fought like sixty to not let him see. He was going to think I was a crybaby like my cousin Freddie Plunkett. He's Uncle Felix's youngest boy, an asshole like his old man. He's about a year older than me. When he was with Peepee and me, it wouldn't be thirty minutes but what he was bawling about something we did to him. Although I guess that time we locked him in a root cellar with a pissed-off skunk was a bit over the top.

Felton looked at me hard, between brief glances at the road, chewed thoughtfully on his wad, and finally said, "Boy, you sure are pushy for a punk kid. What you gonna do if the man at the motel catches you with the dog and says he can't stay? One good whistle and everybody's gonna know we got a dog. We can't tie him up outside by his self. He'll bark all night and keep folks awake. I just don't see no help for it."

I knew my eyes were wet, but like a drowning fool, I hung on so's I wouldn't cry. "If … if he catches me, I … I'll … I know what. I'll tell him I'm blind and he's my Seeing Eye dog. He can't throw us out then. I'll stumble around, you know, make believe, the way me 'n Peepee do all the time. He says I do the best blind man in school."

"That dog's already like your own, ain't he? Tyrane ain't even in the ground and you're talking like he's your dog and all."

I didn't say nothing, but I swallowed a sob.

"You reckon there's room enough in this here cab to play that fiddle, boy?" he asked after reflecting a long time.

The question startled me. "I guess so. Yeah, sure. You want me to play the fiddle while we driving?"

"Can you play it?"

"I can play it some. Tyrane was teaching me. I can play the 'Special,' 'Cotton Eyed Joe,' and a couple of others. I play some better 'n others."

I paused expecting him to say something else, but he didn't.

I asked, "What about Whistler, Mister Haliday?"

He looked at me sharply, I guess 'cause I didn't call him Felton.

"Play the fiddle, boy!" he ordered.

I pulled Tyrane's fiddle out from under the seat, tuned the strings and began to play. As I ran through a few choruses of "Orange Blossom Special," I noticed with a bit of a start that I no longer felt like crying. Soon I was playing that little box like to fill the world with trains, dancers, and rye whiskey.

We were going west, Felton said, which is why the sun was in our eyes late that afternoon. Felton told me it goes down in the west and comes up in the east. I was going to remember that and tell Peepee. He's a smart fella, but I don't think he knows that. I'm gonna wait till he asks me something, acting like he's smarter than me, and then I'm gonna tell him about the sun, where it comes up and all. It'll blow him away!

Felton Haliday was the cheerfullest fella I ever met. Here we were driving the dead body of his best friend to Louisiana, he done almost blinded a irate truck driver that would've killed him if he got hold of him, a dog with us fumigatin' the farmland of three states, and Felton didn't seem bothered a flying flip about any of it.

We pulled into another rest stop for a quick leak, and to give Whistler a break. I glanced into the bed of the truck at Tyrane in the kiddy pool. We had wrapped him in painter's plastic that Billy Bob Hereford—like the cow, you know—took out of his truck and gave us. He called his business, "Billy Bob's House Painting and Expirt Septik Tank Services," which was painted on the side of his panel truck. Billy Bob was less than expert when it came to spelling. The slogan for his business was "We'll paint it or make it flush."

When we started out, there were paint stains on the plastic and you could barely tell what was wrapped in it. Now, however, the rain had rinsed a lot of it away, and you could clearly see Tyrane's eyes and his sparse silver hair. He looked genuinely strange staring out through the plastic and ice water. It made him look like somebody I never seen before, all shimmery like.

We were running out of ice. There was still a thin film of ice on top, but it wasn't going to be long before Tyrane warmed up. Felton said that would not do. I got out the fiddle again and played a few tunes, ending with "Blue Eyes Cryin' in the Rain."

Felton said, "Tyrane couldn't have played that any better, Eldy."

I smiled proudly.

We were getting close to the Tennessee border when Felton cupped his hands to make his voice sound like a loud speaker in a train station and announced, "Next stop Chattanoogy, Tennnnnesseeeeee."

He went on to allow as how "It's gonna be dark in another hour, and

I'm hungry enough to eat a fat mule. Ain't you gettin' hungry, Eldy?"

We hadn't talked much since he said he was going to take Whistler to a dog pound. I was starving, to tell the flying truth, but I was worried that maybe he would say something about Whistler, so I didn't answer. Instead, I shrugged like it didn't make no never mind one way or t'other.

I guess President Eisenhower was a pretty smart fella when he made 'em build these big superhighways. He knew we wouldn't have time to find some place to eat, get gas or spend the night when we was running from Russian hordes, atomic bombs and all, so he made sure everybody put these little signs telling that they was at the next exit. That way, see, you could buy some burgers and fries on your flight to safety.

Felton told me to read signs to him as we come to 'em on account he wanted to make only one stop for everything: eat, gas up and buy ice for Tyrane, and to get us a cheap motel room. He didn't say nothing about Whistler, so neither did I. I had done made up my mind that I would sleep in the truck with him if I had to, to keep Felton from taking him to a pound.

I read all the signs. Seem like there was a McDonald's or Huddle House at every exit and a Motel 6 at most of 'em too. Peepee loved McDonald's. He collected everything McDonald's gave away. It would take a pickup truck to carry all the plastic stuff he's got. He says when he grows up, those stupid things will be worth thousands of dollars, and he's gonna sell 'em and use the money to go to UCLA.

We was almost past the turn-offs to Chattanooga, and the sun had gone down when Felton said, "That sounds just right, a truck stop with a cheap place to sleep and a diner where we can get a cooked meal. They say truck stop food is always good 'cause the truckers are hard to please. But, I think those truckers have iron bellies and would eat fried possum and think it was West Virginia barbecue. I'm sure they'll have ice, though."

He let off on the gas and the Studebaker slowed for the exit.

It was a great big all-things-to-all-folks type place. There was 'most a thousand trucks, I reckon, parked in a paved area near 'bout as big as the football field of the Jupiter Bluff High School Wildcats. Nobody remembers when they last won a game, so most called it Pussy Field, sometimes Pussy Stadium, since we got wood bleachers on both sides and light poles on each end.

There was a motel built by putting boxes in a line with a door to each and then stacking them on top of each other with a narrow walkway on the second floor. Me and Peepee watched 'em build one like it on Cadwallader Street. They throwed it up in less than a week, and a week after that, folks was staying in it.

It looked nice at first, but later the lighted sign only had half the letters lit. For months the sign read, "JUP TE B UFF MOT, but you could get a room for the night or only an hour if you wanted to. Peepee says that was for misbehavin', but I knew he didn't know what he was talking about. How much misbehavin' could you do in an hour?

Right next to the motel was a diner lit up like it was in the middle of a football field, which, in a way, it was. Felton said it looked like it was built when Eisenhower was a West Point Cadet. There was lots of cars at the diner, and you could see people through the windows eating their meals. A group of motorcycles roared in and parked side by side like shiny metal soldiers on a parade ground. The men all wore denim or leather jackets, and all of them wore snake skin boots, and they looked like shaving was a sin. This time, I was sure one of them was the baldheaded rider I remembered from before.

Felton pulled the Studebaker up to the little store on one end of the diner and parked under the bright yellow sign for ICE. He put on his hat which he told me earlier was a "porkpie hat," hitched his pants to loosen them from his skin, and went inside the store.

I went immediately to Whistler, tied the rope onto his collar, and took him to a grassy area beyond the trucks where he ate a can of Kennel Ration. While he was eating, I saw a County Sheriff's cruiser moving slowly around the paved area where I guess he was checking for bank robbers, escaped convicts, or serial killers or something another like that. Whistler romped around enjoying the opportunity to stretch his legs and smell for other dogs. He marked so many bushes that by the time he finished nothing come out but little puffs of smoke when he lifted his leg.

I was strolling back to the truck when I saw the police cruiser make a huge circle around the darker area of the truck parking section, slowing every once in a while to look closely at something.

Up 'til then, it hadn't occurred to me that anybody might question me and Felton about what we was doing. For some reason I started to get a nervous feeling. I got to thinking about what a sheriff might think running up on two fellas in a pickup truck with a body in a kiddy pool of ice.

"Come on, Whistler, we best tell Felton to hurry it up," I said.

I hurried to the store where Felton had just started busting open plastic bags and dumping the ice into the pool. He was enjoying a can of beer while he cut the ends of the bag off where it was twisted together and held by a thick wire.

As I walked up, he said to me, "I couldn't remember how many bags we used this morning, so I bought twenty."

He handed me a skinning knife he took from a toolbox.

"Here, you cut 'em open and I'll dump 'em. I want to get something to eat before we get a room."

I tied off Whistler's rope leash on the other side of the truck, and then as I took the knife, I said, trying to act like it wasn't no big deal, "There's a policeman driving around over by those trucks, Felton. You don't think he's lookin' for us, do ya?"

Felton stopped what he was doing, pushed his hat up a little and gazed across at the truck area. I could tell he was thinking about it, could almost see his mind working. I thought about that trucker with tobacco juice in his eyes and teeth marks in his balls.

As if he read my mind, Felton said, "Most people would call the cops about getting their balls near bit off, but a trucker's not likely to do that. He's probably just checking on loose women hanging out around here. These truck stops are notorious for pimps and perverts of all kinds. He's just doin' his job, I reckon."

We dumped several bags of ice before Felton said, after gulping down the last swallow of beer, "Let's hurry up with this damn ice and get something to eat, Eldy. I'm so hungry, I could eat a whole steer. How's a steak sound to you, boy?"

His confidence was catching. The idea of a sizzling steak and home fries made my mouth water.

"Man, me too! Let's get T-bones so's we can give the bones to Whistler to gnaw on in the truck!"

Then I suddenly realized what I'd said. Like a dippy fool, I had reminded him about getting rid of Whistler. My stomach was suddenly full of a sack of rocks.

I must have looked pretty upset, but Felton just smiled that smirky way and said, downright kindly, "Don't worry about it, boy. We'll work it out."

A few minutes later, a voice said, "How you boys doin' tonight? Looks like y'all come a long way in that antique truck. I ain't seen one of these even runnin', much less lookin' good as that one."

It was the policeman. He had parked his cruiser and now looked at us with arms crossed while he leaned back against the fender of the car next to our truck. He looked to be about fifty, and there warn't no laugh lines around his mouth at all. He didn't seem to have any lips neither. His mouth was just a slit under his nose. He spoke friendly enough, but his manner was like he was deciding whether to squash a bug. He also had a gun the size of a lawnmower.

It was one of them times that Peepee says makes your asshole slam shut, and I'm sure mine done just that. I mumbled what I hope was, "Hello, officer," or "sir," or something.

Felton doffed the hat that made you think of a gangster in the movies. He grinned at the cop like he was glad to see him.

"We're fine, Sheriff. How're you."

Wagging a finger at his truck, Felton responded to the compliments, "Yessir, the old girl brought us a fer piece, right enough. Clean from West Virginny. Been traveling all day, and now me and the boy gonna eat us the biggest steak we can get in that diner yonder."

He chuckled real friendly, way too friendly, I thought.

The cop nodded pleasantly, but I didn't feel no warm welcome coming from him.

"They got good steaks in there, that's for sure," he said.

Gesturing with a wave of his hand, he asked, "What year is the old truck, the fifties or sixties? Studebaker went belly up in the sixties, I think."

The cop's voice was even, like one of my teacher's that used to put me to sleep.

"Nineteen fifty-seven. She's on her second engine, third paint job, and I lost count of batteries and tires."

A voice said, "It's a S–S–Studebaker, s–sir." It was the best I could add to the conversation. In fact, to tell the truth my knees were shaking.

The policeman glanced at me like I was a wart on a cow's butt. His eyes made me think of how mama always knew when I was lying. You know, piercing and sharp, like to look clean through you and see the truth. After a few seconds of looking at me, he studied the four bags of ice that Felton hadn't yet put into the kiddy pool. He seemed to be waiting for Felton to explain, but Felton said nothing. Instead, he turned and leaned on a fender with arms crossed.

The cop waited. He shifted his weight onto his left foot which made his right hip kind of hunch up. I know how stupid this sounds, but I thought of two people dancing without touching each other.

Felton leaned his head back and looked at the cop from under that fool hat. Why'd he have to wear that thing?

Still smiling, he asked, "Is there something me or the boy can do for you, Officer, uh …" he jutted his head forward to read the nametag on the cop's breast, "… Brubaker, is it?"

Arms still crossed over his chest, the cop looked around for a few seconds before nodding and confirming Felton's reading.

"Yeah, that's it, Cogdil Brubaker with the County Sheriff's Department. You can call me Sergeant Brubaker. I just like to see who's passing through, ya know. We don't want the wrong kind of people hanging round out here. It leads to mischief." He toed the top most bag of ice with his left foot curiously, like to see was it alive. His boots were black and spit shined.

"You boys know deer is out of season right now, don't ya? You shoot a deer here in Tennessee this time of year, you go to jail."

He waited for a reaction from us and then asked coldly, "Y'all didn't come up here from Alabamy to shoot y'all's self a Tennessee deer, did ya?"

Felton looked puzzled at Brubaker, then he started to laugh.

"Come up here for a Tennessee deer? Lordy Jesus, no, sheriff. They tell me if you eat Tennessee deer out of season, your pecker won't get hard for a year and the first thing you know, your wife has done took up with a policeman." He paused still chuckling, "Is that true?"

Brubaker hesitated a moment, then laughed also, and seemed to relax a bit, but I didn't think he was through yet.

"What's your name, funny man?" he finally asked as he pushed a cigarette up out of a pack of Marlboros.

He was tall as Felton, who was near six foot his own self, but the cop was a lot heavier 'cause he had a pot hanging over his belt, and old Felton was a beanpole, all knees and elbows, ya know.

The uniform was the most decorated I ever in my life saw. It was pansy blue with gold stripes on the sleeves of his shirt and down the side of his trousers. There was ribbons, badges, gold ropes and name tags and insignias up the bazooty.

"Felton Haliday is my name, Sergeant. This here is young Eldridge Brewer."

He looked at me quickly and there was a message in his eyes that I interpreted to mean, go along with whatever.

"He's suffered a grievous loss and ain't been right since it happened. The boy don't say much, and I think your fancy official uniform kind of shook him up a bit."

Cupping his hand around a BIC cigarette lighter and sucking hard to light up, the sergeant asked, "The way you're talking, sounds like you still got a ways to go. Where you boys headed, if you don't mind my asking?"

Brubaker used his hip to push himself upright and began a slow meander toward the Studebaker. When he was beside the cab, the cop looked inside without even trying to be just curious. He did it in such a way as to let us know he was checking for illegal stuff. I think they call it contrabandaids.

Chapter Five

Sergeant Cogdil Brubaker plucked something from the tip of his tongue like a piece of stray tobacco, but I knew he was showing off 'cause the cigarette he was smoking had a filter.

"I was watchin' y'all from over yonder dumping that ice on something in the back of the truck. Ya might say it kind of sparked my curiosity, ya know? Made me wonder, is what it did."

Little puffs of cigarette smoke that looked blue in the light of the parking lot went with each word when he spoke.

He hooked a thumb at the truck bed.

"You ain't got a illegal Tennessee deer layin' back there, do ya? One with a load of buckshot somebody put in him out of season?"

He craned a look around Felton, who acted as if he didn't know he was in the way and even shifted to innocently block the cop's view even further.

Brubaker wouldn't be denied.

"I think I need to take a look in your truck, if you don't mind. Maybe you could just step out of the way for me, okay?"

His attitude was gettin' a bit ornery, losing what little friendliness it held earlier.

Probably sensing that, old Felton turned up the innocent charm several notches. With a didn't-mean-to smile, Felton said, "I don't mind at all, Sheriff, but don't you need a warrant for that kind of invasion? I mean, I ain't no lawyer, you understand, but wouldn't it be a mess was you to violate our inalienable rights for no reason? I got no reason to say no 'bout you lookin' in my truck, so I ain't saying that at all; but I ain't waiving none of my rights neither. They're inalienable, ya know. That means can't nobody take 'em from ya. If you understand that, you go right ahead."

After a tense wait, he suddenly stepped away from the truck as if it never occurred to him that he was blocking the cop's view.

"Oh, you want to look in it anyway. I'm sorry, I guess I'm in your way," he stammered.

Then to me, he said, "Move out the way there, Eldridge, the Sheriff wants to ignore your rights and gaze upon your dearly departed Daddy, even though he ain't got no search warrant, which is a terrible violation of your inalienable rights. Now don't you go bawling again, you hear."

I first didn't catch his meaning even though his eyes told me to do something. It took only a second though, and I pulled my handkerchief out of my jeans, dabbed at my eyes and broke out into the saddest wail I could muster. I knew I guessed right 'cause a smile came and went on Felton's face.

Me going on like that scared the bejeebers out of Brubaker, and he fell back for a second.

"What's the trouble with the kid? What's he bawling for?"

Felton sighed big and sad, looked up to the heavens and rubbed his eyes. His chin quivered, even his hair looked like the sky had fallen, and he spoke as if holding back a torrent of tears his self.

"It's an awful thing, Sergeant, to have to carry your dearly departed Daddy to his grave in a pickup truck. This poor child has been through an ordeal the likes of which few have ever known."

Felton was goin' on like Brother Cadminster preachin' about sin, which he was dead set against. I thought for a minute he was gonna shout, "Give me an AMEN!"

Getting his wind real good, Felton went on, "Now, here he has to give up a inalienable right so a policeman can see his Pa before proper preparation."

He lowered his head to his chest and sadly wobbled it side to side and then slapped his sides the way Brother Cadminster does when he says somebody's gonna burn in Hell.

He moaned to the heavens, "Oh, the tragedy of it all."

Brubaker's face twisted, mouth twitched with doubt, but he finally gripped the sides of the truck and looked over the rail. It seemed like it was a full minute before it sunk in that it was a dead man staring at him through painter's plastic and a million ice cubes.

Myself, I thought Tyrane looked nice in the kiddy pool with them green, red and yellow smiling fish, happy turtles and dancing crabs and all, like one of them little aquarium castles in the dentist's office.

Brubaker's eyes popped wide, and his jaw dropped open. He looked like a person in the funny papers, you know, when his hat jumps straight up. His jowls fluttered the same way his cheeks do on his other end when they expelled air.

"My God, there's a dead man in this truck!"

He stepped back from the Studebaker, but I guess he still couldn't believe it, because he jerked himself against the truck to look again.

He shouted, "He's covered with ice! There's fish and turtles. My God, it's … it's a kiddy pool! There's a dead man lying in a plastic kiddy pool!"

Felton explained quickly, while trying to maintain a sad attitude.

"Yeah, well it was the only way to keep him on ice for a long drive. The fish and turtles are a nice touch though, don't you think? Eldridge's friend, Peepee Ping Pong let us have the kiddy pool. It don't leak or nothing."

Brubaker began clawing at his pistol. He pulled at it twice before remembering to unhook the safety loop that kept it from falling out in the car.

I was bawling as loud as I could. A crowd had gathered, and as it grew larger, I cried that much more. Felton made a big show of patting my head and telling me not to cry, that it would be all right.

"The nice officer," he said, "would not think of interfering with the proper interment of a boy's dear departed Daddy."

Felton added, real loud for the crowd to hear, "Especially without a proper search warrant, after the boy had gone through so much to be with him at his final hour!"

Felton put his hands up in protest when Brubaker drew his gun, but I don't think it scared him that much. He soothingly said, "Be easy, Sheriff. There ain't no cause to get excited. There ain't no reason for firearms just because you crucified this boy's inalienable rights."

Brubaker was excited, and I think he was scared, too. He must have thought he was facing two bloodthirsty serial killers or at least dangerous desperados. He was scared that he might have broke the law, too. His voice got higher and crackled, "P–p–put your h–hands up! You're under arrest."

He pointed the gun at Felton first and then at me, 'cause I let out a wail like a dying elephant.

"You got a warrant for that, too?" Felton asked innocently. "You sure as shootin' don't want to stomp on another inalienable right, you know."

A woman in the crowd started laughing real shrill. She was all painted up with thick red lipstick, and her boobs threatened to jump out of her low-cut blouse.

She hollered, "Will that gun go off, Bru baby? The one you had out for me earlier didn't have no bullets, and you couldn't aim it!"

The crowd laughed and hooted like crazy.

Someone else asked, "Did you put in that bullet they gave you to play with, Brubaker?"

Brubaker spun around, shocked to see the crowd that had gathered— truck drivers, traveling strangers who had stopped for a bite to eat, and a number of painted, hard-looking women that Felton told me later were prostitutes. When Felton started to speak again, the sergeant spun toward him, then back and back again. Somebody yelled that he was gonna screw himself into the pavement.

The bikers were there, too, hanging back from the rest, just watching the whole thing. A few of them had helmets, but all wore something leather—jacket, pants or both—and snakeskin boots so much alike they might have been uniforms.

Felton started to say something, but Brubaker got down like a crab and stuck the gun out in front of him holding it in both shaking hands.

"G–get 'em up, I said. D–don't move. Don't move."

He fumbled at his belt a few seconds, I guess for some handcuffs. His face was white as a sheet and sweat poured into his collar turning the blue material near black.

"One of y'all g–go to m–my car over there and get my handcuffs. These are real dangerous men I've got here."

He released the gun with one hand and with a shaking finger pointed at the Studebaker. "Th–there's a dead man's body in a kiddy pool in th–that truck. It's got fish and turtles, too!" he said to the watchers.

A woman asked with a giggle, "Are the fish and turtles dead too?"

Nobody moved. Instead, they grinned at each other and at Felton, who was trying not to grin. One man's eyebrows arched and he mouthed the words, "Kiddy pool?"

I heard somebody in the crowd say, "Dangerous men? C'mon, Brubaker, hell's bells, the boy couldn't be no more than twelve years old. What's the matter with you? Listen to what the man has to say."

Felton said, "We ain't serial killers, Sergeant. That there's this boy's Daddy, who choked on a chicken bone the very day he seen his son for the first time in 'most ten years."

Then Felton turned to me and said, "Tell him, Eldridge. The poor police officer is beside his self with worry, him having already committed a sack full of serious inalienable rights violations."

We got Brubaker calmed down some, and the threat of a lawsuit for violating our "inalienable rights" did a lot to diffuse the confrontation, but we weren't anywhere near out of the woods yet.

Felton said appeasingly, "Look here, Sergeant, me 'n Eldridge are hungry. Why don't the three of us go in the diner yonder, sit down in one of them booths until things are a little calmer, and order up a steak? It'll be my treat, and over steaks and home fries, I'll tell you the whole story. C'mon, be nice. When's the last time somebody whose rights has been stomped on offered to buy you a steak? You can see we ain't armed. What's the harm?"

I thought for a minute that we were home free, but I was wrong. Brubaker said he had to radio for backup, and I pictured an army of policemen swarming on top of us with pistols and shotguns and tanks and swat teams and all the stuff me and Peepee used to play like.

Brubaker said, "Maybe y'all ain't desperados, and maybe y'all are, I don't know. There's a dead man floating in a kiddy pool there, and I mean to find out what the hell's going on."

He had stopped pointing the gun at Felton and me, but he still had it in his hand. He waggled it at us, but I had an idea he liked the thought of a free steak.

"Come with me over to my cruiser, while I radio in and get some help out here." He paused. "That ain't gonna add any more inalienable rights violations, is it?"

Me and Felton exchanged looks, and I could tell he was really worried too. It was the first time I had seen that look.

"Well, I ain't so sure about that, Sergeant. If you're arrestin' us, don't you have to make some speech about a lawyer and keeping silent and words held against us and all that stuff, like if we ain't got no money, y'all will hire us a lawyer? Hell, it's a list those cops on TV read from both sides of a card. It must be a foot long, ain't it, y'all?"

He directed his question at the crowd of now about thirty people, some of whom had looked in the truck.

The woman who said Brubaker's gun didn't have no bullets answered, "You damn straight, mister. He reads that card to me every time he arrests me, near ten times at least. O'course he never takes me in. It's a temporary arrest, you might say, till I pay my special fine, say, about ten minutes or so."

Several in the crowd snickered, and a woman blurted out, "If he lasts that long!" Brubaker's face turned beet red, and he went to blustering and shaking his head.

Felton turned back to Brubaker.

"Can't you call your headquarters from the diner to talk to a lawyer, Sergeant? I don't think I can stand much more of this boy's carryin' on, no matter how justified the child's grief might be, ya understand."

I cut loose with another good wail, and I heard a whistle, but I guess we were upwind, and I didn't smell nothing. But I started getting me an idea.

Brubaker seemed like a bully in a cop's uniform, and he didn't seem very smart. He also acted scared that he just might be in trouble. His eyes had the gleam of somebody who couldn't push away from the table when there was still dessert left. I had seen that in Aunt Bessie's eyes too often to mistake it. Also, I'm sure as flying apples, he was worried about the stuff Felton was throwing at him. I think that's why he went for it.

He said, "Well, I guess I can do that. I don't reckon it'll make no never mind if we all had a steak while we sort this business out."

"Yes sir, Sergeant. I knew you were way too shrewd about trampling on inalienable rights to talk about something so complex on a scratchy radio."

Brubaker nodded his agreement and started to holster his gun, hesitated, and waggled it at us saying, "Y'all remember now, I'm real good with this thing, so I don't want no funny business in there. Somebody could get hurt was you to try something stupid." He harrumphed real big. "Y'all go in front of me."

I felt like I was being led to a wall to be shot like they do prisoners in movies about Mexico. Really, we weren't any better off. It didn't matter what story Felton told, we did have a dead man in the back of a pickup truck. Felton smiled his smirky smile at me to buck me up, but he was worried, and I knew it.

In the long day together, I got to thinking that there wasn't nothing that could stop Felton Haliday, that he was one of those kind of people that would always come out okay. He would always think of something, some way out of a pickle, like with the truck driver. I didn't think he could finagle his way out of this mess, though, so I concentrated my thinking real hard on an idea that was flickering in my mind. Peepee says I can come up with some real doozies. I hoped he was right, cause if I didn't, I was afraid we were in a mess of real doodoo!

We ordered big t-bone steaks. The sergeant glared at us from across the table in a booth, not quite as hostile as before, but not exactly warm neither. I guessed a ten-dollar steak didn't go far in Tennessee.

He lit a cigarette, leaned back and looked down at us from across the table.

"All right," he said, "let's hear how come you to be carrying this boy's daddy floating in a kiddy pool of ice. Now don't go lying to me. I've heard all the lies there is to hear. First off, how come him to be dead? What, or maybe I ought to ask, who, killed him?"

I interrupted Brubaker. "I got to go to the bathroom, Felton."

I looked hard at him to let him know I was lying, but I didn't know whether he caught on.

"You go ahead, boy. Wipe your face with some paper towels, too. You look red in the face. I know how it is when somebody walks all over your rights and all. Some cold water will make you feel better."

Felton turned to the sergeant and said, "He's a fine boy, Sergeant. I just don't know how he could bear up under the grief he's had to endure, and now there's this business of his rights getting walked on by a policeman who we may have to sue."

Sergeant Cogdil Brubaker glared at me, but made no objection.

I hurried to the men's room. As soon as I was in there, I spotted the window over the toilet stall. It had been painted and would be hard to get open. I got on the water tank of the toilet and tried it anyway. It didn't budge a dadgum whit. I took my pocketknife and hacked at the paint along the window edge. My fingers were sore as boils by the time I got it cut all the way round. I hammered at all four sides of the window and hit up at the edge of the top with the heel of my hand. It was loose, but the window didn't move much.

This is taking too long, I thought. I was sweating hard and worried that the cop would come to check on me.

Grunting like I do playing football, I pushed up with all my might. The window slipped up about an inch. I saw a broom in the corner and used the handle to pry it the rest of the way open.

I wasn't sure the opening was large enough, but I had to try. By angling myself corner to corner, I managed to get my upper part through, but then it seemed like I was stuck, and I got pretty scared. I wriggled this way and that for what seemed like an eternity, but I stayed stuck.

I swear, I thought I'd never get loose, but finally I felt some movement. My hip scraped, and I knew I had left some skin on the windowsill. It burned like blazes! My shirt tore, but suddenly I came loose and almost fell on the pavement outside.

In the parking lot, I ran lickety-split to the Studebaker, untied Whistler and hurried over to the cruiser, praying all the while that it was not locked. Policemen always tell you to lock your car, but most of the time they don't lock their own cars, like nobody's gonna break into theirs.

Whistler was glad for the attention, and I hurried so he wouldn't waste his best whistles on me. Thank the angel of bad boys, the police car was open, and Whistler, who never passes up a chance to ride in a car, jumped in the front seat full of piss and vinegar and, I hoped, whistles. He showed his enthusiasm with a fine whistle, and I messed with him a few seconds to add to his excitement. Then I closed the cruiser's door.

I ran back to the window and found an old milk crate to stand on. Back inside, I splashed water on my face and wet my shirt to look like I spent a long time washing up. When I got back to the table, Felton was talking about how my daddy had spent three months in South America trying to rescue me from kidnappers, which, he said, as I sat back down, "turned out not to even have poor Eldridge. You can imagine his disappointment."

"What did he do then?" asked one of two waitresses who had stopped to listen to the tale of my courageous, but dead, daddy.

Brubaker had listened to Felton's story, obviously not buying it, but he had cooled off a bit. He said, "Well, I ain't sure all that's true, Felton, (Using Felton's first name seemed like a good sign to me) but I'll buy it for right now. I gotta call my office and get some advice about hauling dead bodies across state lines. Y'all sit right where ya are, unnerstand me?"

Felton said, "Yeah, sure, go ahead. You need to ask about inalienable rights violations, too, Cogdil. You probably ought to talk to the lawyer y'all's county uses when a citizen files lawsuits for millions of dollars. Something big like that, you don't want him to find out in the newspapers. That'd piss him off, I'm sure."

Brubaker's face twisted with worry for a minute, and then he seemed to shake it off. He slid his fat butt out of the booth and went to a wall phone, where he stood with his back to the wall so he could watch us.

I said in a whisper, "Felton, listen. Send me to the truck for something, anything. Then wait about two minutes and make a break for it. I'll have the truck started."

Felton whispered back, "It won't work, Eldy. Even if I made it outside and got the truck goin', the old Studebaker wouldn't be no match for that police car. He'd catch us before we got a mile down the road. Just sit tight. I'll think of something."

"We ain't got time, Felton. If he gets more cops here, we gonna be up that creek— you know which one I'm talkin' 'bout—without a paddle. We could be stuck in Tennessee for a week."

"Eldy, listen, I'll think of something. I can at least get you clear. You're under age and all."

I noticed Brubaker's face get dark, like he suspected something, and I got a little frantic. "Felton, damn it, listen to me. He won't chase us, Felton. I put …"

The sergeant hung up the phone and started walking back to the booth muttering about the phone being busy. He looked at me like he thought I crapped in his corn flakes.

Felton was surprised at me cussin' like that, I reckon. I begged him with my eyes while he was talking to the approaching Sergeant.

Felton said, "I reckon if that's what's worryin' you, how Eldridge's daddy died, Sergeant, we'll get papers and show you what the Jupiter Bluff authorities had to say about it. Eldy, how about you run out to the truck and get that folder I stuck in the glove box. You know the one marked Coroner."

Under the table, he pressed the truck keys into my hand.

I breathed a huge sigh of relief. I knew there wasn't no folder, but to give Whistler as much time as possible, I asked Felton, "You talkin' 'bout the one that the coroner and the sheriff gave you when we left out this morning?"

Felton snapped his fingers and confirmed, "That very one, Eldridge. That very one."

"Yes, sir." I turned a teary eye at Sergeant Brubaker. "Is it all right, Sheriff?" I asked like Brubaker was Miss Hurlbutte in school and I had to go to the toilet.

"I ain't the Sheriff, boy." He answered irritably, "I'm one of his deputies, a sergeant in the Sheriff's Department. Yeah, go ahead, but don't be all day."

I trotted dutifully to the door and slipped out. I ran to the cruiser, got the dog out after exciting him for a few seconds and quickly closed the door. I put Whistler in the back of the truck, threw the last bags of ice unopened into the kiddy pool and got in the driver's seat. I put the truck in neutral and had to stretch way out to get my foot to the starter on the floor. The first time I tried, I couldn't press it down far enough, but I extended my sneaker as far as I could. Thank the angel of mischief, the engine turned over and the truck started right up.

I started to get out, but along about then, the diner's door flew wide open and, yelling for me to open the door and clamping his porkpie hat on his head, Felton come hotfooting across the parking lot like his ass was on fire. Right behind him came Sergeant Brubaker just a cussing and trying to get his pistol out again while he scrambled down the steps. Felton ran as fast as Peepee did one day when Mister Blackford chased him with a shotgun when he caught him stealing watermelons.

I slid over and Felton jumped into the driver's seat, slammed the Studebaker in reverse, backed up, put it in first and shot across the parking lot to the highway. Brubaker finally had his gun out, but I think he forgot to release the safety. I heard a string of vile curses, but no shots. He ran to his cruiser, jumped in and pealed out of the parking lot to the highway. He didn't go a hundred yards before he slammed on the brakes and skidded into a ditch alongside the road. The car ended up with the front end sticking up and its headlights lighting treetops across the highway as if the car was taking off into the wild blue yonder.

Brubaker staggered, gagging, from the cruiser. He frantically fanned his hands before his face like a man swatting a swarm of bees. He weaved away from the open car door coughing and throwing his guts out. I swear it looked like a cloud of yellow-green smoke boiling out of the open car door. After that night, I figured dog farts were a yellow-green color, but you can only see 'em when there's a whole lot of 'em.

Chapter Six

Felton laughed like yesterday's tomorrow and hollered, "Yeehaw!"

He pushed the Studebaker up to top speed—ninety-five or so on the speedometer—and we raced off into the night.

"I bet even that fat bastard's uniform smells like dog shi ... uh, pookey."

He cackled some more.

"Did your daddy teach you tricks like that, boy? If he did, he was one very smart guy."

My mood swung instantly from happy and satisfied to anger.

"No!" I snapped, "I don't have a Daddy. My Daddy's dead. He didn't have time ... I mean, we didn't have a chance to ... My Daddy's gone!"

I stared out the truck's window at the mileage markers going by.

Felton lost his grin and looked at me kind of funny, but he didn't mention Daddy again and was silent for quite a while.

We weren't but fifteen or twenty miles from the Tennessee border. On the "cold war highway" again, Felton flicked on the dome light and told me to get out the map and find a route through the country to Alabama or Georgia.

"Whichever we can get to the quickest. We're right where Georgia and Alabama get together to form the rest of the South."

He said it would be best if we got off the big highway for a while.

"I figure it'll take old Sergeant Cogdil Brubaker quite a bit of time to get any kind of pursuit started. That cruiser will need a week's airing out. A man couldn't stay in it more than a few minutes before he'd OD on Whistler's environmental contribution. We could be in Alabama by that time. Still, it'd be better was we to stay off the big highways."

"Won't he use his radio to put out a PTA on us?" I asked, 'cause if it come to a poke in the eye or tell the truth, I was still scared.

Felton chuckled, "APB is what you mean—all points bulletin. Well, he might, but I don't think so. The fact is I think he believed me when I told him we had papers explaining how Tyrane come to be dead. He was more worried about civilian rights than anything else."

Felton bit off a chunk of tobacco, chewed at it till it got soft and then went on, "I don't reckon there's a whole lot of cops had to deal with somebody taking a dead body across state lines, and I kept asking him if there was such a law, like I doubted that there was. He didn't have no idea and was thinking about lawsuits if there wasn't one. Everybody was already laughing at him. He was scared that we were gonna sue him. Now, a dog has rendered his cruiser environmentally stunk up. Naw, Eldy, old Cogdil don't want to humiliate his self any further by pursuing this matter."

I saw on the map that if we stayed on the road we were on when we left the truck stop, we'd come to a state highway that crossed over into Alabama. With the dome light on, I showed Felton the route and he agreed that was the best thing to do. "It'll take a little longer than the Interstate, but I think that's how we ought to go."

We drove along in silence for about ten minutes before I remarked, "I sure am glad that's over."

I pulled my tee shirt up to check the scrape on my hip. It was raw and red with little flecks of blood, worse than strawberries I got playing baseball, but it hurt like a hundred devils.

"Me too, Eldy. Me too." He glanced across at the angry blotch of skin. "How'd you get that strawberry? It looks like a mean one."

"I got stuck in the flippin' window in the bathroom. I thought I was gonna be there 'til Chicago Cubs won the World Series and we was gonna end up in jail sure as a pig don't fly." I didn't want to let on how plumb really scared I was.

"Well, Eldy, we were up the old creek all right. There just ain't no other way to put it and just to be straight with you, boy, I didn't have no idea how to get out of the mess we were in."

He spat a stream of brown stuff out the window, thought a minute and added, "I should've known that a boy old Tyrane took to was the kind that would come up with something. You okay?"

I didn't say nothing and we rode in silence for a while.

"Felton."

"Yeah, boy."

"I was scared. My … my mouth was so dry, I …"

"I know. You did good, Eldridge Brewer. You did real good. Tyrane would have been proud of you."

He didn't say anything more for a few long minutes then he added, "Your Daddy would have been proud of you, too."

A sign loomed out of the dark in the headlights.

WELCOME TO ALABAMA

"I'm still hungry. Let's get something at that little eatery we saw on a sign a while ago," Felton said, changing the subject. "It should be coming up soon and maybe they know a place we can stay the night. We can get something to put on your strawberry too."

It wasn't the steaks we had planned on, but a big old plate of eggs 'n grits and country sausage, stacks of pancakes and toast was almost as good. We ate at a place called Mama's Best Plate Forward, ten or fifteen miles inside the Alabama line, on State Highway 75, what Felton called a "two-lane blacktop."

I figured the big bony woman that cooked the eggs and sausage was "Mama" 'cause she ordered two younger women around like they was slaves or something. One of the slaves was really nice. She said she had a boy about my age, but I didn't think so on account I'm big for how old I am.

I said around a mouthful of sausage and grits, "I'm twelve, but most folks want me to be fifteen because I'm so big and not as old as I look."

She was pretty in a sort of worn kind of way. She had blonde hair, but it come from a bottle I knew since her eyebrows was black as a crow. Her eyes were big and round like marbles and she had pretty boobies that seemed to want to get out and wave at you. I liked talking to her even though she kept throwing glances at Felton. I think she was making eyes at him.

She smiled at me real nice from her side of the counter and told me, "My boy is a little older than that. He plays football for the high school. Do you play football?"

"Yes ma'am, but I'm only in the seventh grade and I can't play for the Pussies yet. I'm gonna be a running back on account everybody says I'm greased lightning. Peepee—he's my buddy—says I might win the Hightman trophy. That's the one they give for being the fastest football player ever."

Felton looked down at me from his counter stool as if I just pulled a big old nasty booger out of my nose and wiped it on my shirt.

"What?" I demanded, not knowing what I had done wrong.

Face a little dark, he said, "Who are the 'Pussies'? That's not very nice, Eldy."

"Well why not? They're the Jupiter Bluff Wildcats but they never win any games so everybody calls them the Pussies. What's wrong with that?"

I don't understand grown-ups sometimes, what in the bibbity bop was wrong with "Pussies"?

The girl behind the counter giggled as if I said something naughty, like callin' her boobies something worse.

It gave me a fit to get yelled at when I ain't said nothing bad. I protested too. "They been calling Jupiter Bluff teams the Pussies for as long as I can remember, Felton. That's not what they call the girls softball team for some reason. They call them the wild kittens because they win sometimes. I don't know what you're goin' on about it for."

Felton's face turned red, embarrassed I guess.

The girl was trying not to giggle, but for a flying fig, I didn't know what was funny.

Felton held up a hand, laughing. "Okay, okay, Eldy. I didn't know. Forget it, okay?" He smiled, tolerating me being wrong. "You were talking about the Heisman Trophy, Eldy. They give it for the best football player in college every year."

"Well, I'm gonna do that when I get big."

"Sure."

He turned back to the girl. Offering his coffee cup, he asked, "Can I have some more coffee, Miss, uh …"

Still a little giggly, she said, "Pattie. It's Pattie. I'm kind of a transplanted Yankee. I'm Pattie Pearl Penrod."

Felton chuckled. "And I bet you're from Pittsburg, Pennsylvania, right? Let's see, Pattie Pearl Penrod from Pittsburg, Pennsylvania."

Pattie Pearl started acting cutesy-pooh. You know what I mean, as girls do around the gym when we're playing basketball.

She squealed, "Why, how'd you know tha-at? That is just amaaaazin' to meeyee." She cut her eyes, "Somebody told you, didn't they?" Her eyelashes flickered like the girl skunk in Pepe Lepew cartoons.

Felton's face reddened too. He twinkled a grin at her and replied, "It was just a lucky guess."

She was actually flirting with Felton, who might one day be my Mama's boyfriend. Well, I mean, if things go … Anyway, she was flirting with him and him mixed up in carrying our friend thousands of miles and all. She could mess us up flickering her big eyes at Felton. I had to put a stop to that.

"My friend's name back in Jupiter Bluff is Peepee." I said loudly, trying to break up the flirting. "He's a Oriental and he knows judo, kudo, karate and all those k and o fighting things you see in the movies. I seen him break a board with his bare hands once, only it broke his finger."

Felton grinned at me, but Pattie Pearl Penrod flashed me a quick look before saying to Felton, "You're new around here, aren't you?"

I stuck my finger out in front of her face.

"Right here. This finger here. Now he's always shootin' people the bird all the time. See like this."

I showed her how Peepee's finger sticks out funny, but she didn't pay me no 'tention cause she was makin' goo-goo eyes at Felton, the witch!

Ignoring me like I was a tree frog on her front porch, she went on, "I don't think I've seen y'all around here."

Her eyes never stopped flashing and then she leaned on the counter which got up under her boobies and pushed 'em up 'til I thought they would spill into Felton's pancakes.

I wanted to kick him in the shin under the counter when he missed his mouth with a hunk of pancake, being so hung up looking at her boobies.

"I'll be gettin' off soon, if you'd like me to show you around town. It's a little town, but it's real nice, and," she fluttered her eyes at him, "there are a couple of things to see. Do you like to dance?"

I jumped in real quick.

"Peepee scratches his head like this and shoots the whole class the bird. Miss Hurlbutte, too. I used to laugh like a flyin' hyena."

Felton looked at me puzzled, but said to Pattie Pearl, "Well, that's mighty kind of you, Pattie Pearl. We're from Jupiter Boob, uh, Bluff, West Virginia, on our way to Louisiana."

I decided I had to end this blooming romance right now.

I said, "We're taking Tyrane to his funeral down there. You know, where he can be with his long-lost girl."

I twisted so she had to notice me.

"Oh, I'm so sorry. Are you Tyrane?" she asked Felton.

Before he could answer, I beat him to it.

"Nah, he ain't Tyrane. Tyrane's out in the truck with Whistler. We didn't bring him in 'cause he'll whistle like crazy getting excited about comin' inside and all."

"Uh, Eldy, you don't need to tell her all that. We, uh …"

Pattie cut him off.

"You left your friend in the truck outside while y'all ate dinner in here because he whistles? That doesn't seem very nice."

Felton started to explain. "No, Pattie, you don't understand. He couldn't …"

"Whistler is our dog." I jumped in. "I done fed him 'fore we come in."

Felton rolled his eyes at me.

Pattie asked, "Well, where's Tyrane?"

"He's on ice in a plastic kiddy pool," I announced quite proudly.

Pattie's eyes got bigger, if that was possible.

"Why is he in a plastic pool of ice? He'll catch his death."

"No, he won't," I said. "He's already dea—"

"Eldy, that's enough."

Felton was right perturbed now.

"What?"

"We have to go. How much is the bill?"

"What? What?" I asked again.

Pattie said, "Well, I … I don't understand. I'd like to meet your friend. Aren't you going to bring Tyrane in for something to eat?"

I wolfed down my last sausage, and chugalugged my milk. It was all I could do to keep from snickering.

"He doesn't need anything, all right? What do I owe for dinner?" Felton snapped. He looked real worried, but shoot, I couldn't let that wicked witch get my Mama's boyfriend. Well, almost boyfriend, anyway.

It was awful quiet in the truck. Felton was Pissed at me, I could tell. Mad was oozing out of him like stuff between your toes in the chicken

yard. I sat scrunched against the door wishing I was in the back with
Tyrane and Whistler.

I don't know how far we went before Felton finally said accusingly,
"You did that on purpose. I know you did."

"Whaaaat? Did what?" I asked.

Man, I used all the cuddly little boy charm and innocence I could
scrape up, but I didn't think it was gonna be enough, 'cause he was
pissed.

"You started all that crap about Peepee and his broken finger. What
was that? Broke his finger on a board and shoots people the bird all the
time now? Harumph! That was bullcrap, Eldridge Brewer." He spat out of
the truck's window. "I bet Peepee ain't got no broken finger at all. Karate!
God all-mighty!" He rolled his head and stared at me accusingly.

I didn't argue with him. Peepee did hurt his finger trying to break a
board with a karate chop. He didn't break it, but all day he looked like
he was giving me the bird. So, I gave the story a little extra punch. It
must have worked 'cause Felton Haliday didn't get mixed up with no big
boobie waitress and maple syrup.

Felton waited for my answer and when I said nothing, went on, "You
didn't have to tell her about Tyrane and Whistler. What was that all
about?"

I started to giggle 'cause this picture started forming in my head and
it got funnier and funnier and I just couldn't help it.

"Now, what the hell are you tittering about, Eldridge Brewer?"

I reckon I lost it sure enough then. I laughed even harder.

I was laughing so hard, it was all I could do to tell him, "I thought for
a while, Felton, you was gonna jump over that counter and put your head
between them boobies and go brrrrrrraaaaaach and get maple syrup in
your hair!"

I tried to stop laughing but I couldn't, 'cause I could see Felton's head
dripping maple syrup. I laughed so hard my stomach started to hurt.

For a long minute, Felton looked angry but as he stared at me, he started to smile. After a bit, he started laughing, too, and soon we was both belly laughin' like two fools. Between belly laughs, he said, "Well, Eldridge Brewer, I'd be lyin' to you if I didn't admit I thought about it real hard."

After a second, he laughed even harder and added, "You know what, Eldy? Maple syrup will never taste the same to me."

I guess I had enough cuddly charm after all.

A few minutes later, we found a motel that I swear made me remember that old horror movie where some guy thinks he's his own mama and kills folks in the shower. I even looked to see if there was a haunted house on a hill behind the motel. There wasn't but it might as well have been. What was there was a miniature golf course that looked like it hadn't been used in years. Grass had taken over the little carpeted greens and the cartoon clown was as scary as the haunted house in the movie. I shivered thinking about a murdered body inside the faded orange windmill.

The motel was called the DEW DROP INN. It was a two-story building in a big horseshoe with rooms opening over a swimming pool that was surprisingly clean and sparkling in the lights surrounding it.

There weren't more than ten or so cars there, and I guessed there were even less on the backside where there were more rooms. We stopped in the overhang of the office where Felton went inside to get us a room. I followed him after I gave Whistler reassuring fondles behind the ears.

Felton went up to an L-shaped counter with a silver bell on it. Seated there was the check-in fella, but you could only see him if you leaned over the counter.

He was a dark-complexioned foreigner. In fact, I wasn't at all sure he was from our planet.

Felton hit the bell to get his attention and said, "We need a room. How much is a double?"

The clerk looked up from some kind of ledger book he was working on, stood up and answered, "Yssir?Howmaninyourparty?"

Felton looked puzzled.

"I said we need a room. How much for a room?"

"Fortydollahdooblehowmaniyoourpartee?" He smiled politely.

He talked real fast with a Martian-type accent. You had to strain to hear him much less understand a flippin' thing he said. The man put emphasis in all the wrong places, you know, everything seemed like a question. New York cab drivers in the movies talk the way he does. Peepee would have called him "a interplanetation visitor."

Felton looked at me as if I could help. I had no idea what the man said either. I shrugged, "I don't know."

The martian was looking at the glass door and said, "Youhvedog?No dgs?Cnthaverim?Odg?"

I didn't want to, but I told Felton, "I think he's asking about the dog."

Felton pointed to me. "Blind. He's blind. That's his Seeing Eye dog. His dog to see—get around."

I immediately started to act blind. I knocked the little bell on the floor and felt around to find it.

The Martian shook his head. "Nodgsloud." He started to turn away. "Yougonodgsloud?Goelswhere."

Felton looked around until he found a sign posted by the entrance to the rooms. He stepped over to it and brought it to the clerk. He held it out to him and pointed to the section regarding handicap accommodations.

"You want me to call the blind police? You could go to jail for fifty years treating a blind person this way."

The man's eyes grew big as saucers. He might not understand this handicap business, but police he knew. He said fearfully, "Nopliceyouhaverim.nochahg?Rimoneohfour?Youtake.Yougomorrow. Noplice."

He pushed a key into Felton's hand, continuing to mumble, "Youtak ekeystaygomorrow?"

Felton had to force himself not to smile. He looked sternly at the key and then nodded.

"Okay, Mohammed. No police." He took the key, tossed it up and caught it.

To me, "C'mon, Eldridge, take my arm." He stuck out his elbow and I slipped my hand in it.

"Can I keep my dog?" I asked pitiably. "I can't see without my dog."

Felton patted my hand sympathetically, "Of course you can. The man just didn't understand."

I did a job of blindly crashing into the door on the way out that would've got me a starring part in a Hollywood movie.

I walked Whistler in and out of the room a few times so that he wouldn't get excited and whistle a happy tune about being inside. It seemed to work just as Tyrane once told me it would.

Felton brought in a large leather suitcase with a brass nameplate stamped with FH. I went out and got the cardboard box Mama taped a handle on for me. It said Del Monte Tomatoes on the side in big green and red letters. I unfolded the flaps, dug around for my pajamas and then when I pulled them out, I wanted to just crawl under the bed. Mama automatically packed my favorite pajamas in my "suitcase." They are too small by a whole lot, but it was the little pink teddy bears that turned my face scarlet.

I saw Felton look at me and my "Teddy" pajamas. Sweat popped out all over me. I felt blood rush to my face and then my face catch fire, burning like a flying volcano. I wanted to run for the bathroom and drown myself in the toilet.

Felton smiled understandingly. "Mine had rabbits on 'em," he said thoughtfully. "I wore 'em 'til I was 'most fourteen and they were hardly more than rags. I'd be wearing 'em now 'cept I couldn't get 'em on, I expect."

I wanted him to know I wasn't no sissy, so I said, "Well, I don't wear these no more. Mama just forgot. She screwed up and put the wrong pajamas in my box is all."

I shook my head as if to say I couldn't understand my Mama making such a awful mistake.

"I ain't wore 'em since I was little, but I reckon they'll have to do. Probably won't even fit. I don't know since it's been so long since I wore 'em. First grade, I think."

Felton didn't say nothing else, just went back to doing whatever it was he was doing. In a second, I realized he was unwrapping the suit that Aunt Bessie said was Tyrane's but he hadn't worn for as long as she could recollect.

Noticing me watching, Felton said, "I thought maybe we ought to take a look at his suit, Eldy. I think it's been put away for a long time and we wouldn't want to get to a funeral parlor and ain't got no fittin' suit for Tyrane."

He snipped the last piece of scotch tape and the brown paper fell away.

It was a grey suit, with little tiny white stripes like the New York Yankees uniform only lots darker. He set the pants aside and picked up the coat, which buttoned across itself—one flap buttoned over the other flap like the end of a Christmas package. Felton said it was a double-breasted jacket but I think he was mixed up 'cause Tyrane didn't have no boobs. I thought not to correct him though, on account he looked so alarmed.

"Damn! De-double damn!" cried Felton, "This ain't gonna do. What would Leona think of Tyrane coming back to her looking all moth-eaten like this?"

"What's wrong, Felton?"

"Lookit here in front, Eldy. The damn moths done ate tracks all across the lapels." He shook his head. "Eldy, we can't bury Tyrane in this suit. We'll have to buy him another suit tomorrow. We'll ask Muhammed where there's a store where we can get a suit."

I laughed, thinking how there wasn't nobody gonna see him but me and Felton, and I ain't never seen him in a suit before anyway. I didn't think it made no never mind at first till I thought of the words to the song about meeting blue eyes up yonder where there ain't no parting and strolling hand in hand again.

Nosiree bob, we sure as shootin' couldn't bury Tyrane in a moth-eaten suit.

"You want me to ask the Martian in the morning where there's a store we can get a new suit at?" I asked.

"You're supposed to be blind, remember?"

"I remember, but I want to see that Martian's face when he sees I ain't blind."

Chapter Seven

I don't know when a shower felt so good. I stayed in it till my skin tingled all over. When I came out Felton was layin' on the bed with a beer and the telephone snuggled in his beard 'tween his ear and the pillow. At the foot of the bed, Whistler was sort of lying down whilst slurping beer out of a plastic bowl on the floor. Felton smiled at me without a smirk or wisecrack about my pajamas, which was a dadgum good thing if he wanted to see tomorrow.

I didn't know what he was talking about, but he quickly changed the subject when I came out of the bathroom. I sort of wondered if he might have been talking 'bout me when he looked up. He acted like he wasn't, but you can't fool me, even though he went on like he was talking about where we were.

"… a little town in Alabama."

Felton put his hand over the mouthpiece. "Did you see a name for this town, Eldy? I don't remember seeing one."

I laughed and said while waving a folder around, "We are in—ta da—Crossover, Alabama, where they have a annual," I opened the colorful brochure that I snitched from the lobby and began half reading it, and half acting like I was reading it, "Eggplant Festival. It's a Extry … Extra-vaa-ganza. They're gonna have all kinds of stuff, it says here."

I opened the folder and started reading some of the events.

"Let's see now, for the kids there's a eggplant hunt gonna be held on the lawn of the New Alabamy Bank. The winner gets to take one eggplant home." I giggled thinking about it. "Everybody else has to take two. They pick an Eggplant Queen and all too. They got the Eighth Annual Eggplant Casserole and Bake-Off tomorrow. They're gonna bob for eggplant on Saturday night and," I gave a big flourish with my hands, "they're gonna have the Annual Booby Eggplant look-alike contest!"

Felton put his hand on the phone. "The what?"

I pretended like I was still reading, "Booby Eggplant Look-alike Contest. It says Pattie Pearl Penrod from Pittsburg, Pennsylvania, is the hands-on favorite to win the Golden Booby!"

I cackled crazy like at Felton, the way old Coocoo Corky on my ball team does. He puts straws in his nose and jumps around goin' "romph romph" as if he was some kind of walrus.

It took Felton a few seconds to stifle his giggling and waved me to be quiet and said into the phone, "We are in Crossover, Alabama."

He paused, listening.

"I know but we got off the main highways. It seemed like the thing to do. No, no, no trouble, uh, we just thought it best, you know."

The person on the other end of the line talked a good bit and then Felton responded, "I enjoyed it too. A lot." He sounded like he was talking to a girl.

Watching him talk on the phone and tryin' not to spy on him, I realized how little I knew about Felton Haliday, exceptin' him bein' a friend of Tyrane. I didn't know him at all, really. For example, who was he talkin' to on the phone?

I felt really stupid. What was I doin' thinking about him and my Mama maybe being sweethearts. He might even be married, have a passel of snot-nosed kids or something and go home when all this was over. We didn't mean nothin' to him. We were just a bunch of strangers in a dumb little town in West Virginia. I ain't got no hold on him, me just a snot-nosed brat myself.

I don't know why I was gettin' so down in the dumps. What was I thinkin', him and my Mama? Shoot, he'd leave in a few days and then it'd be just me and Mama and Punky, and I'd hear Mama crying late at night again.

I threw the brochure about the Eggplant Festival on the floor.

I don't know when I missed my Daddy so much as I did that night watching Felton talk on the phone. For some reason it made me mad.

Felton talked for a long time, keeping his voice low. I was glad because I didn't want to listen to him talking to a wife or girlfriend or maybe one of his kids or something.

I swallowed hard, slipped into the bathroom and changed my pajamas for my dirty drawers. Felton was so busy runnin' his mouth on the phone, he wouldn't have noticed if the whole damn Miami Dolphins football team walked naked through the room.

Felton didn't see me slip outside with Whistler. The dog jumped in the pool as if he'd been doing it all his life, and I found a stick we could play catch with.

About a half hour later, Felton came out to the swimming pool and sat down on one of those metal chairs with plastic bands laced to form the seat.

"You're takin' a kind of chance, ain't ya? If Mohammed came out here, even he could see there ain't nothing blind about you," he said. While he fondled Whistler's wet ears, he watched me close.

I didn't answer at first, but then I muttered, "I don't care," and dove to the bottom of the pool so I wouldn't be able to hear what he said. I came up and swam to the opposite side with my back to him.

He called, "What's wrong, Eldy? You act like you're pissed off at me."

I didn't answer him, on account I was mad at him, but to tell the God's own truth I didn't have no idea why.

I thought about Peepee and wished he was here. If he was here, I thought, I don't know, maybe I wouldn't think about Mama and Felton or Punky or Daddy.

What was I doin' here? I didn't know why I came with this stranger, Felton Haliday, anyways.

"Well, are ya?" Felton called from across the pool.

I sniffed, climbed out of the pool on the far side and grumbled, "I think I'll go in now. The damn pool is too cold to swim in anyhow. The stupid water's too flyin' cold and I got to dry off Whistler 'fore I go to bed."

I didn't even know if he heard me, and in a funny way, didn't care. At the same time, I cared a lot. A whole damn lot!

Damn them for takin' my Daddy! Damn them to hell!

I ran to the room, went inside and closed the door. As the door closed, I heard Felton call, "Eldy, come talk to me. Eldy!"

I took my wet drawers off and quickly slipped on my teddy bear PJs. Felton was coming in the door when I crawled under the covers in the bed nearest the bathroom and pulled the sheet over my head. I kept my hand out to touch Whistler so he could make what was hurtin' feel better.

Felton said, "Eldy, if I don't know what's wrong, I can't fix it. All of a sudden, you're acting like I got the plague. You want to talk about it?" The other bed squeaked and I knew he was sitting on it looking at the lump under the covers that was me.

You can't fix it. Nobody can fix it. Mama's been lonely and sad all the years my Daddy's been gone. How you gonna fix that? Me and Ethel are company and all, but it ain't the same and it ain't never gonna be the same. How you gonna fix that?

Shit! I mean shingles! No, damn it, I mean shit!

I remembered one night I was layin' in the bed thinkin' about how to snap off my curve ball to that fat kid that plays for Bickford Street. I was thinkin' if I started it way outside, when it broke across the roof shingle (that's what we used for home plate), Fatstuff'd swing like a girl. It made me laugh, but then I heard Mama cryin', and I knew she was thinking about Daddy. I got up, went in her room, and crawled in bed with her.

I told her, "Don't cry, Mama. Me and Punky are here. Everything's gonna be all right, you watch and see. Don't cry." She hugged me and said she was all right, but I knew she wasn't and that my getting in bed with her helped only a little.

I woke up in the dark motel room and couldn't get back to sleep, thinkin' about Tyrane and Felton, Mama, and I don't know what all.

There was a clock screwed to the table so's wouldn't nobody run off with it. It said it was quarter to three in the morning. Finally, I got up and slipped outside by myself. Whistler gave me a curious look, but I told him stay and quietly closed the door behind me.

It was so dark and quiet by the pool it should have given me the flying willies, but it didn't. The dull roar of an occasional eighteen-wheeler's great big old engine cut the quiet into before and after. I could hear tires hiss along the pavement and kind of thrupple over seams in the concrete near the motel.

I sat on the edge of the pool, dangling my feet in it and tossing loose pebbles across the water, not really trying to skip them like I do at the pond out back at home.

I didn't hear Felton come out of the room, so I don't know how long he was out there before he said anything. I almost crapped in my PJs when that crackly voice of his broke the stillness.

He said as if we had been talking a while, "I've always had trouble sleeping in a strange bed. I get to sleep all right, but then I keep waking up, you know?"

He sat in the grass by the pool, extending his long legs toward the water and watching his wiggling toes. He handed me a Dr. Pepper and took a long pull on one of his own.

"I see you have the same trouble, Eldy."

I didn't say nothin'. Truth be knowed, I don't know what I thought and so I didn't know what to say, so I didn't say nothin'.

"Sometime getting up, moving around like this helps."

I took a big swallow of the Dr. Pepper.

"You miss home?" he asked.

I thought, can't nobody fix what's wrong. I shrugged.

"No, not really. Well, maybe a little."

We was both silent. We stayed like two statues ceptin' when we drank from our sodas.

I asked suddenly, "Do you think my Mama is pretty?"

For the first time since he sat down, I looked at him closely, watched him.

He answered quickly, almost as if he knew I was gonna ask him that.

"Nearly 'bout as pretty a woman as ever I saw."

I didn't say nothin' for a long time. I didn't really know what to say, watching him so close like I was. I heard a dog bark off in the distance, but it was too far away to be Whistler.

Finally, I asked him, "Do you like my Mama?"

He looked me straight in the eye, stared at me and then nodded his head. He didn't smile like some people do when they just shootin' off their mouth.

"Well, Eldy, I do," he said real serious. "She's quite a woman. She runs that farm by herself and all. That takes a special woman to take on something that big, you know. She obviously is a good Mama if her son and his sister are any indication. She's a good woman, pretty too."

I sipped some more Dr. Pepper and didn't say nothing. The distant dog barked again.

"She cries sometimes in the middle of the night," I said after a minute. I found another small stone, skipped it across the water and then added, "It's Daddy, I think."

Felton nodded his head solemnly.

"Yeah, that's probably it. She misses him something awful, I'm sure. It's tough to lose your mate, Eldy. You never really get over it. You learn to live with it, but you never get over it."

I took a pull on my Dr. Pepper, and poked my finger through a hole in the knee of my pajamas.

I said, stating a fact, "You ain't said nothin''bout no family, Felton."

"Don't have one."

I looked at him like I wasn't sure he was tellin' all the truth.

He sighed and went on, "Eldridge, you have a way of poking into things better left unpoked into."

He was silent, pulled on his Dr. Pepper. I noticed a shadow behind his eyes like the one I first saw there in the living room at home.

I watched him but didn't say anything on account I knew he wasn't gonna leave it like that and I wasn't gonna let him. I sensed it was painful for him, but I couldn't make myself stop staring at him, forcing him to talk.

"I had a wife and son. They're gone now."

I could see the pain in his eyes as he talked, and I started to feel like a roach. You know, scratching like that at a man's sore spot.

He sighed heavily. "I ain't always been the perfect citizen you see now, Eldridge. There was a time when I couldn't get enough whiskey, women and mischief and it cost me the only things worth a damn in my life."

"I'm sorry, Felton. I shouldn't have asked, 'specially since it ain't none of my business. I just thought that, well, maybe that you and Mama ... Don't pay me no mind, I'm just a bippity-bop fool kid. You don't need to tell me."

He chugalugged the rest of his Dr. Pepper and said bitterly, "They gave up on me picking 'em up at a movie one night and caught the bus to come home. I was drinking and had forgot. A drunk driving a rattletrap logging truck hit the bus, knocked it off a bridge. They found 'em after dragging the river for three days."

I wanted to crawl in a hole making him talk about it.

"I wasn't worth a damn for a hell of a long time," he continued. "Tyrane was in prison, our band was gone, and Leona LeSeur was dead. My guitar and banjo were gone, I didn't know where, and I didn't care if I lived or died."

I sniffled against a full little-boy cry. The dog barked again and another big semi shished on the nearby highway.

I said after a while, "Sometimes I miss my daddy so much it hurts. Sometimes it hurts so much I can't stand it."

I tried to explain. "He was took from me, see. He didn't die like Tyrane … like … like a man ought, ya know? He was took! It hurts so bad sometimes."

He murmured, "I know, Eldy."

He put his arm around my shoulders, a little bit like Daddy used to do when I hurt myself. I put my face against his chest, and it all spilled out of me. For the first time since mama got the telegram, I cried over my daddy.

The next morning was one of those mornings when you wanted to run to the top of a hill and holler as loud as you could, "Ain't it a good day for Eldridge!" It was dry, warm, breezy, and every bird in the world was singing its favorite song. I felt like a big weight was gone off me and that I was the luckiest boy on earth.

I took Whistler for a walk behind the motel, and then me and Felton pretty well emptied out the motel's icemaker filling up the kiddy pool.

Before we left, I made it my business to go by the tiny lobby of the motel just so the Martian could see me being led by Whistler. I used a long length of rope and groped around behind him as if I couldn't see nary a thing. I don't know what that alien thought when he seen me wobblin' crazily behind my "Seein' Eye dog." I knocked over the newspaper stand, tourist brochure rack and everything else not nailed down. Peepee would have been proud!

The Martian pushed open the door for me but I just crashed into it, reeled aside and said, "'Scuse me, the dog don't rightly know where the hell he's goin'."

Whistler obliged with an explanation of his own.

I was laughin' so hard by the time I got back to the room Felton thought I was crazy as a drunk chicken.

"Now what the hell have you done?" he asked.

"I run me a wing-dingy on that foreign goofball who give us our room last night," I answered between peals of laughter. "You should've seen his face when old Whistler cut loose one o' his better farts, and I crashed into the rack where they have all those folded things about places to see and things to do in Crossover, Alabama. He probably never saw a blind man get dragged thataway by his Seein' Eye dog."

Fortunately, we were already pulling out of the parking lot when the Martian came to complain about the blind boy and his dog. 'Course maybe he wasn't going to complain, but tell Felton that the Seeing Eye dog was gonna get his boy killed.

We fed Whistler and gassed the Studebaker at the service station up the road from the motel. The clerk there told us there was a shopping center with a big store called Mega-Mart in it a few miles south. Felton allowed as how maybe we could get Tyrane a new suit there.

We ate breakfast at the golden arches—my suggestion, but mind you, not 'cause I liked it, but so Felton wouldn't get tempted by another pair of bouncing boobs. Felton said we would make it into New Iberia early enough to go to the funeral home if we didn't waste a lot of time diddlin' around.

The shopping center wasn't much to look at. It had a great big concrete parking lot that looked big enough to hold every car in Alabama. The question was why anybody would come there in the first place.

In the middle of a line of smaller stores was the Mega-Mart. Among the little places was a pizza joint called Alfredo's, a shoe store that claimed the lowest prices in Crossover and an eyeglass place with a pair of eyes staring out at the parking lot. Some kids had done a fine job of painting them to look cross-eyed. I admired it and gave some hard thought to where Peepee and me could find us a sign like that.

Felton parked the Studebaker away from the rest of the cars, so's wouldn't nobody look in the back and fill their britches when Tyrane looked back at 'em through the plastic and ice and little green frogs. We hadn't been bothered by people looking back there 'cause old Whistler had been taught that "on duty" meant that he was to kill and eat people who stick their noses where they ain't got no business. Whistler takes his duty downright personal. He looks like a loveable teddy bear till he growls and shows his fangs, and then he looks like a grizzly bear with a toothache. Anybody diddling around the back of the Studebaker hears a fearsome growl that'd tighten their butt real fast.

An old geezer in a crinkly blue suit greeted us near the line of shopping carts in Mega-Mart. He smiled as if we was long-lost grandsons returned from the North Pole.

"Good morning, shoppers. It's wonderful to see you today. Welcome to Mega-Mart." he said it almost like a song and with a sweep of his hand like those women do on The Price is Right.

Felton stopped beside him and asked, "How about pointin' us to the men's department there, Mister. We got to buy a man's suit."

Mama says these Mega-Mart stores hire old folks to act as greeters, which was what this man was for. He looked at Felton, blinked his eyes and smiled all over again till it was big as Texas and then said to Felton confidently,

"Good morning, shoppers. It's wonderful to see you today. Welcome to Mega-Mart."

I wondered if he had a son clerking at a motel.

Felton tried again, louder this time. "Where's the Men's Wear Department? That's what we need to find, sir."

The greeter looked confused, but only in his eyes. I thought the smile was stitched on his face by a doctor. He could've been runnin' for his life as the store burned to the ground and would still be smiling and saying, "It's wonderful to see you today. Welcome to Mega-Mart."

Felton started to shout, "WHERE IS THE …?" paused, shook his head and said, "Aw, the hell with it."

I guess it's time for me to admit that I'm not near as perfect as I seem. I have a few ways that my Mama says are "hiccups" in my personality, which is her nice way of saying that I sometimes piss her off. The thing that gets her pawing the ground at me is when I get in a store with a lot of good stuff. And Mega-Mart has a lot of good stuff.

We started weaving our way between counters of groceries, women's underwear, pots and pans, microwaves, coffee makers and about a million other things when we chanced upon the sporting goods section. I detoured and said I'd catch up with Felton in a minute. I wanted to look at the new glove Spalding come out with that spring. My old one was getting shabby and the padding was gone in the pocket. Even Peepee's sorry fastball stung now since my glove had got so thin.

In the sporting goods section, I found it was the only glove in a box. I took it down from the shelf, opened it and slipped out the most beautiful golden leather baseball glove God and Spalding ever made. It was signed on the thumb by Ozzie Smith, the Wizard of Oz, who could turn a double play quicker'n a greased eel.

Man, it was pretty. It wasn't tan like them other gloves. It was gold as the McDonald's arches, soft and bendy and felt like it was made for my hand. There wasn't no baseball in the world that could get by me with that glove on my hand.

I popped my right hand into the pocket smartly a half dozen times, got down in my shortstop squat and hollered down the aisle, "Hey, swing batter, batter, batter. You're mine, fat stuff."

I thought of that fat kid from Bickford Street with each pop of my fist in the glove. He hit a ball past me one time and I ain't never forgot it. "Right here, baby!" I cried and swiped the glove near the floor like snagging a hot grounder.

"That's a fine glove, boy. A glove like that could make you an all-star."

I turned around and found a long-haired guy in a dirty leather jacket watching me practice my moves. His smile showed the ugliest, crookedest teeth I ever did see. With his yellow staring eyes and them crooked buckteeth, he made me think of a dead possum.

I said real confident like, "I'm already an all-star, but I'm gonna get me one of these soon. Soon as I cut enough grass. I was just testing it, you know?"

I began trying to put the glove back in the box the way it was.

It scared me the way he looked at me and then around the store as if to see if anybody was watching him. He reached out for the box, but I jerked it away from him and snapped, "I can do it. I don't need nobody's help. My Daddy is over in the plumbing department buying great big lead pipes, he'll help me if I need it."

He grinned at me like his poop don't stink and mine does. He said, smart-alecky, "Yeah, your Daddy just went in the rest room. Let me look at that glove. Maybe I'll buy it for ya."

The grin turned sour and evil. I could feel my knees start to shake a little.

I don't know how he knew who I was, and that I was lying. I figured something was bad wrong, and when I saw his boots I knew it. How in the flying snakes could it be that I seen them snakeskin boots three times? I thought about making a run for it, being as how I'm so fast and all, but I saw a fat, mean-looking biker in a red polo shirt and wearin' the same kind of boots at the other end of the aisle. He watched me while he picked his teeth with a sliver of wood.

Crooked Teeth dropped the nice guy act and said hoarsely, "C'mon, boy. I know where your friend is. I'll take you to join him. There's something we'd like to discuss with y'all. You come on with me now."

He took a tight grip on my upper arm that hurt as he dragged me toward the other man. I still had the glove box open and the glove in my hand. I looked, but there were no clerks and, apparently the sports section wasn't high on the list for Mega-Mart customers in Crossover, Alabama.

Chapter Eight

Crooked teeth said with a vicious sneer, "You make a peep, you little snot, and I'll stick that glove up your butt. You walk beside me, you hear?"

I felt my butt hole scrunch and my belly tighten into a knot. He reached again for the glove, but I held it away from him.

"Oooow, you're hurtin' me. What do you want?"

I thought about what he said and realized that they must have Felton, too, and took him to the men's room. I was scared, ya know, but, it was just like with Cogdil Brubaker at the restaurant, I wasn't gonna let it make me do nothing stupid. I decided I would play along till I knew what these assholes was up to.

I could see the rest rooms were over by the return and complaint counter where customers bring back all the junk that don't fit, don't work or they just don't want. The bikers pushed through a crowd of women at a table in the center of the aisle that was piled high with blouses. Above it was a sign with a purple smiley face.

Up to 70% Off Marked Price.

The women must've thought the bikers were trying to beat them to the best prices and didn't back up a bit. I could see Fatty was gettin' mad, 'cause his jaw worked like he was eating the words he wanted to say.

To my right was where they sold electronics stuff, and there was about a hundred TVs turned on. I didn't pay no 'tention at first then something caught my eye on a talk show and I started gettin' me an idea. In the meantime, just for the hell of it, I dropped the glove box, grabbed a bright blue and yellow blouse a big horse-faced woman had in her hand and showed it to Crooked Teeth. You'd of thought I found the gold at the end of a rainbow the way I hollered out real loud and kind of sneery, "Here's one! Mama would love this one, Daddy! It'll look good with that black eye you give her last night!"

The woman whirled, snatched it back, ripped the ball glove off my hand, and snarled at Crooked Teeth like a dog over a ham bone.

"Go find your own sale, mister, and tell your snot-nosed brat to keep his damn grubby hands off my blouse!"

Boy! I tell you, I wouldn't want to tangle with that woman. She probably eats her young!

Crooked Teeth snapped back, "Blow it out your ass, lady!"

Fatty didn't seem to notice. They just kept dragging me toward the men's room, but the incident gained me a second to snatch something off a counter.

By this time, I knew they weren't looking to rob us. I figured out that they had been following us since Felton tobacco-juiced the truck driver. That was the first time I saw the snakeskin boots. They probably lost us when we ran out of the truck stop last night. Also, they must've known we were going south too. They could have found us only by running down the few roads we were likely to use. It didn't take a whole bunch of smarts after that to find us in a Studebaker truck like ours.

As we passed the grocery section, I tried as hard as I could to look for things that I could use. My plan was coming together in my mind but I didn't want to do nothing till I actually saw Felton.

The aisles were narrow and every ten feet or so there was a stack of something on special like a microwave oven. There was a REGULATION BASKETBALL for seven ninety-five. I had one of them once and that's all the dadgum thing was worth.

Fatty didn't go in the men's room with us. He stopped outside to act as some kind of guard, I guess. Most folks would rather pee their pants anyway than go to the toilet in a big store like Mega-Mart. Peepee says perverts and serial killers hang out in them all the time but I never seen any. One time I saw a shifty-eyed fella in the bathroom at Walgreen's. He had great big rabbit teeth and wispy gray hair. I kept my eye on him whilst I peed just in case, but he didn't make no pervert moves or anything. I was scared then too, but I didn't let it get to me.

In the men's room at Mega-Mart though, it almost did. Two big men wearing leather biker britches and ragged denim vests had Felton in a corner. He was holding himself up by pressing the flat of his hand against the tiled wall. There was a gash over his eye and a purple bruise on the other cheek. Blood ran from the gash into the corner of his eye and down through his beard and into his shirt collar. Since he was a little bent over, I figured he took one in the belly, too.

The bigger of the two men was heavily bearded and stunk like a horse that ain't been out of his stall in a coon's age.

He said, "All right, Felton, is it? Here's the deal. Turn that junk truck you're driving around and go back to Saturn Bluff or wherever the hell it is you came from and big boy outside won't make the kid his girlfriend."

He gripped Felton by the shirt front and sneered, "He's already told me he would enjoy spending some time alone with him, if you get my drift."

Felton's tongue licked blood from the corner of his mouth. He leaned back against the wall and wiped the blood from his eye. He was woozy, unable to focus, but his mind was sharp as ever. He said thickly between groaning breaths, "Right now, Mister, you stand a decent chance of surviving this. But if you harm that boy, even tweak his ear, you better kill me, because I'll kill your whole damn family. I mean your mama and daddy, your kids and your dog, too. The ones that are already dead, I'll dig up and kill again and then I'll track you down and peal your skin off."

I recognized then that he was talking to the biker that pulled alongside us yesterday.

The man laughed, "Man, you ain't in no position to ..."

"Do whatever you got to, son of a bitch, but remember what I said," Felton muttered and shook his head to clear it.

The other guy, a bony fella with a crew cut and greasy skin, backhanded him.

I strained against crooked tooth's iron grip on my shoulders.

"Stop it, you bastard. Stop it!" I shouted. Snorting like a bull, I twisted back and forth against the strong hands gripping me.

Crew Cut laughed as Felton struggled to stay erect. However, Crooked Teeth relaxed his grip on me just a little.

I whined to Crooked Teeth, "If you don't turn me loose, I'm gonna crap on your shoes, you idiot. I'm trying to go to the toilet there." I pulled in the direction of the nearest stall.

Stinky turned from Felton and said, "The little snot ain't goin' nowhere, let him go to the toilet. I don't want to hear his mouth no more."

I hollered at Stinky, "You stink like a three-day-old run-over possum, asshole. If you could smell yourself, you'd puke!"

Stinky whirled around and raised his hand to belt me, but Felton managed to mumble, "God help you if you do it!"

I honestly think it was Felton's warning that saved me from a bad beating, because Stinky lowered his hand and told Crooked Teeth to let me go to the bathroom.

As soon as I got in the stall, I moved fast. I undressed, except my tennis shoes. Damn, it was cold in that air conditioning. I was gonna leave on my jockey shorts, but that would give the bikers something to grab, so I shed them, too. I packed my pants around my feet as if they were pulled down, opened my pocketknife, and then the thing I snitched off the counter. In a few frantic minutes, I was ready.

I stared at my hands and said a prayer to Mama and the only saint I had—Saint Peepee Phing Phong of Jupiter Bluff, West Virginia. Would you believe my hands got steady as a rock? Well, I won't say they did then, 'cause they was shakin' like a leaf in a spider web.

I pulled the latch back, picked up my pocketknife, took a deep breath, and hit the stall door with my shoulder as hard as I could. The door sent Crooked Teeth reeling across the tiled floor. The two facing Felton spun and grabbed me one by my hand, the other by my shoulder, while Crooked Teeth righted his self and wrapped his arms around me.

Them big bad bikers had no more chance of holding on to me than an elephant has to fly. I squirted out of their hands the way a minnow does when you're tryin' to put him on a hook. I was naked as the day I was born and slick as a catfish with Vaseline smeared on me from asshole to appetite!

With Stinky's attention diverted, Felton hit him with a roundhouse right to the side of his head. In the meantime, I went for the bathroom door, jerked it open and plunged outside.

Fat stuff heard the commotion and was there to head off whichever one of us came out of the door, but he sure as a flying tackle didn't expect a wild, naked two-legged greased pig to come out. I plowed full into him with my head down and slashed at him with my little pocketknife. I wouldn't have been sorry if I cut him real bad, but I suppose it was best what happened.

As I came out of the bathroom door, I screamed so loud, I would've won the Jupiter Bluff Hog Callin' Tournament hands down. I yelled, "Help, help, they tore my clothes off! Pedalfile! PEDALFILE!"

That was what I heard the fella on TV talking about, you know, men making little boys do awful things. The fella called them "pedalfiles", although I don't know why.

I keep my knife razor sharp. The blade caught some flesh I think, but not much. Mostly what it caught was Fat Stuff's pants and belt, slicing right through 'em. Fat Stuff grabbed me, slipped off, and then dove for my legs, which is when I got his pants. I was still yelling "Pedalfile" as loud as I could as I squirted out of his grasp and took off running naked up the main aisle of Crossover, Alabama's Mega-Mart.

ON ICE ■ 95

Fat Stuff got to his feet but immediately went sprawling across the floor when his pants fell down around his ankles.

I swear I don't know where all the people came from, but suddenly there was folks running all over the place led by the horse-faced woman, her face red with rage.

When the good folks of Crossover, Alabama, saw a naked, terrified, screaming, but otherwise sweet little boy runnin' through a store chased by a bunch of snakeskin-booted, scraggly-bearded, hairy-shouldered bikers with long greasy hair and smellin' like a manure pile, they became a lynch mob. A mob that was even scarier for being led by a pissed-off horse-faced she-bear who was near 'bout as big and muscular as the bikers. John Wayne might have beat the Germans, Japanese and 'bout a hundred Indian tribes, but even he couldn't have stopped that mob.

The big woman ran up to old Fat Stuff and pounded him on the head with a spanking new gigantic frying pan. Each mighty blow pealed through Mega-Mart like the gong of St. Mary's Cathedral in Jupiter Bluff.

The other bikers came out of the men's room and ran smack into enraged women armed with everything from heavy fishing rods to toasters, anything they thought they could use to pound into mush the perverts chasing that cute little naked boy. And punish them they did! One woman near 'bout wore out a biker with a toilet plunger.

This one huge black guy, who could have been a linebacker for the Washington Redskins, seen me running from the bikers and I never saw a man so mad about anything in my life. He didn't run toward them, he walked with long, angry strides, fists clenched, and when he got to Crooked Teeth, I thought of the song about "Big John" where the singer sang, " … a crashed blow from a huge right hand sent a Louisiana fella to the Promised Land."

Two or three well-meaning folks tried to grab me, but with no more success than the bikers. I hollered that they hurt my Daddy in the bathroom. "Help him!" I cried and pointed.

One of the bikers, I think it was Crew Cut, tried to go back in the bathroom to escape a woman with a shovel. He disappeared for a second and then reappeared back-pedaling from a straight right hand to the face from Felton, who followed him out with his fist drawn back. When the biker turned around to run, the woman bounced the shovel off his head.

The mob around the bikers pulled Felton away from them, clucking sympathetically at his bleeding face. They figured he was injured defending me from the pedalfiles. It enraged them even more that the evil pedalfiles hurt my father, too, and the mob pressed their attack on the bikers with renewed enthusiasm.

Felton caught up with me somewhere around the candy section, snatched a tablecloth off a table and threw it around me. We made a beeline for the exit.

As we passed the greeter at the shopping cart stand, the old man smiled at us like his store hadn't turned into World War III. He seemed not to notice that the area by returns and customer service was full of men and women hurling curses and Mega-Mart stock at four bike riders, one of whom had lost his pants and was nearly unconscious.

Although I ain't absolutely sure he seen us, the old man smiled big as all outdoors in our direction and cheerfully told us how glad he was that we shopped at Mega-Mart today.

We raced across the parking lot, piled into the Studebaker and put Crossover, Alabama in our rear view mirror as soon as we could.

On the road again, I reached back of the seat for my suitcase/cardboard box and struggled into jeans and a tee shirt. I got my clothes on and then, suddenly I got scared. The fear I wouldn't let myself feel before come on me the way the spirit come on brother Timrod in the church one Sunday, 'ceptin' I didn't holler Halleluiah. I couldn't help myself. I just started shaking and couldn't stop.

Felton pulled into a rest area. The next thing I knew, I was sitting at one of the picnic tables and old Whistler was licking my face. Felton had cleaned himself up and sat across from me sipping one of our Dr. Peppers.

"You want one?" he asked.

I nodded. A few minutes later, he put one in my hand. The cherry flavor seemed to calm my nerves a bit.

Felton looked me straight in the eye and said, "Eldridge Brewer, you may be the bravest boy I ever in my life seen. I'm privileged to be with you."

Felton allowed as how it'd be hours before the mess at Mega-Mart could be sorted out, and with us not there to press charges the bikers would eventually be let go. The thing is, what in the flying frogs was it all about?

Felton was sitting on top of the table with his feet on the seat. He bit off a chew of tobacco and said, "Well somebody sure as hell sicced 'em on us. One of 'em kept talking about Tyrane bein' a jailbird and don't nobody want him in the cemetery with decent folks."

"Ain't that what Uncle Felix called Tyrane at the house? A Jailbird?"

"Yeah it is. He was pissed off and that's a fact, but it don't make sense that he would go to the trouble of hirin' a biker gang."

"I don't think so neither, Felton. He's a asshole right enough but I don't believe he'd do nothing like that. He ain't nothing but a fart in the wind, been sellin' junk cars fer twenty years. He acts as if he's a big success, but Aunt Bessie says he ain't got a pot to pee in, ner none to throw it out. He ain't got money to hire no biker gang."

Felton thought about that for a long time and finally declared, "There's only one person I can think of that would do such a thing: Leona's brother, Edwin Jr. He hated me, but he hated Tyrane more because he was everything Edwin LeSeur wasn't and probably never could be."

"Is he a biker, Felton?"

"Oh no, he ain't, and that's what's botherin' me. First of all, how'd he know we were coming, and I don't see how he could hook up with a biker gang hundreds of miles away?"

I took a long pull on my Dr. Pepper and poured some in a plastic bowl for Whistler. He loved Dr. Pepper almost as much as he did beer.

I shook my head and said, "I wouldn't put it past Felix Plunkett to call somebody down there, seein' as how mad he was when he left, but he wouldn't know Leona's brother."

"There wouldn't be many LeSeur's in New Iberia. One or two phone calls and he'd get him easy enough. But I still don't see how LeSeur could hook up with the bikers. That just don't figure."

"I do, if Uncle Felix called him. Mama says he runs off for days at a time with a bunch of bikers. Freddie—that's his snooty youngest son, he's a crybaby—told me his daddy puts on leather pants and a helmet and runs around acting like one of them Hell's Angels. Maybe, he put Leona's brother onto some of them."

"Well, that would certainly account for the bikers. LeSeur's got enough money to hire two biker gangs if he wanted to."

"Yeah, well he better do that or git his self an army then, 'cause I'm buryin' Tyrane next to Leona LeSeur, and can't nobody stop me!"

"Us, stop us."

"Yeah, us."

"Why don't you play us a couple tunes on the fiddle, Eldy? It'll help me think."

The day was warm and sticky and I could smell rain too. There were no dark clouds, but my nose is always right when it comes to rain. Sure enough, after a while, I noticed raindrops on the windshield, no more than a light drizzle and soon I saw the prettiest rainbow I ever in my life saw. It was like some giant artist painted the prettiest green and pink and yellow arches in the world.

Mama took me and Punky to church every Sunday morning, and I did try to pay attention in Sunday school. Well, most of the time anyway. My Sunday school teacher was a spinster lady name of Madeline Lucretia Fitzwaller. "Mad Madeline" was a spittin' image of the wicked witch of the west and I thought she might drop a house on me if I didn't pay attention. Her face looked like a prune with teeth and eyeballs, and when she laughed, it'd curdle your breakfast milk. She read the Bible and then told us what it said like we didn't hear her read it in the first place.

Brother Cadminster was bad about that, too, when he got going full bore on sin. There's only ten commandments but that preacher added a lot more from thou shall not dance to thou shall not eat meat on Fridays, shoot marbles in the front yard or have a pillow fight on a sleep over. I didn't think the Bible said nothing about swatting Peepee with a pillow.

Anyway, the rainbow made me think of God. I never bought all that stuff Cadminster said about Him. You know, about smitin' us for thinking evil thoughts and all. Rainbows proved there is a God because only some super-being could do that. God is nice too. How could anybody mean make a thing as pretty as a rainbow?

He knows we're gonna screw up, but He's our friend and likes us. What more is there? We got to try and do right. We owe Him that. We don't need commandments to know what is wrong or right, you know? Well, anyway, that's how I looked at it. God is good and I tried to be.

For the next couple of hours, we drove hard, "pushin' the envelope," was the way Felton put it. The little Studebaker liked the superhighways, the way it purred. Once Felton chuckled and said, "I believe my old truck likes your fiddlin', Eldy. Seems as how it's hummin' right along with ya."

It didn't at first occur to me, but as I played "Cotton Eyed Joe" I realized that playing the fiddle had calmed me down. It was strange. When Felton talked about dropping Whistler off at a dog pound and I got so worried, the fiddle helped then, too. It was like my old friend Tyrane was guiding my hands on the bow the way he used to out by the chicken house in his backyard.

I couldn't count the hours we used to sit back there, me on a cut-off tree stump and him in that old rocker. I'd sing along when he played, and he'd do the same when I played, and then we'd both sing together.

He had a voice a little bit like Johnny Cash, only Tyrane's was, well, you know how water rills and burbles over stones and stuff in a stream? That was Tyrane's voice, sweet as a mountain spring. As we drove on amongst all those people going God knows where, I knew I could hear that voice in my mind anytime I needed to.

No sir, nobody could stop me burying Tyrane next to Leona LeSeur.

We drove for a long time not talkin'. Felton sang softly whatever I chose to play. My bow arm got tired, so I put the fiddle back under the seat and settled down for what was still a long ride yet. Raindrops began beading on the windshield again and when they ran together, Felton turned on the wipers and they set up a flap-flip rhythm.

Felton said, "We still got to get a suit for Tyrane, but I reckon we can do that when we get to New Iberia. I spent many years there and I suppose a lot of places I knew are still there. There's a place down near the Quarter where we used to buy the outfits we wore when we performed. It specialized in show business get-ups. All the top musicians used to go there: Fats Domino, Pete Fountain, Bobby Rydell, Chubby Checker, even old Lloyd Price bought some of those gaudy things he used to wear from Sol's Fine Clothes. I ..."

"I never heard of those people, Felton, 'ceptin' Fats Domino. Mama said she and Daddy used to dance to a song about Blueberries."

"Blueberry Hill. A great record. A great song, too." Felton reared back and sang, sounding like a voice I had heard on the radio before. The singer sang through his nose and pinched the words.

Along about the third line, I hummed the familiar melody, and remembered Mama used to hum it when she was fixin' supper. It made me feel sad and good at the same time.

Chapter Nine

"Why now, Felton?"

"What?"

"Why now? You hadn't seen Tyrane in years. Why now? Why'd you come see him now? Why not, I don't know, last year or the year before that?"

"It just seemed like the right time, Eldy."

I didn't say nothing for a long while. Something must have made him come all the way from Minnesota to Jupiter Bluff, West Virginia, I thought.

"Felton?"

He kept his eyes on the road. Even under the brim of the porkpie hat, I could see the shadows in his face deepen. He had told me about losing his family and all, but those sad shadows I saw in his eyes so often, I had thought they were from long ago. Now, I somehow knew something had happened more recently.

"When did it happen, Felton?"

"When did what happen?" he said sharply, with his eyes looking troubled and his lips curled downward.

I held my tongue because he knew what I was asking and I was determined to wait him out. I don't know what made me think then of Leona LeSeur, but she came to my mind and a thought suddenly bounced around in my head like a swished basketball on the court after a free throw. Did he and Tyrane part when Leona LeSeur died? He said that Tyrane went nuts, started drinking and then robbed a liquor store and went to jail. But he also said he lost contact with Tyrane. When did they part?

"I don't like talking about … it was a while ago, all right?"

The basketball bounced less and less. Something came between Tyrane and Felton and drove them apart. That seemed clear to me. Every slap of the windshield wiper seemed to hit me in the face as it began to dawn on me.

Leona LeSeur!

I threw it at him high and hard, accusing him.

"You loved her too, didn't you?"

I could see the guilt on his face. It was the same kind of guilt I felt every time I thought about them taking Daddy to fight in a war. You wanted to do something violent, kick a tin can, stomp a bug, or just jump up and down, but you didn't do those things 'cause it'd be stupid. But when you felt that somehow you caused some kind of evil thing, it showed. It showed because it hurt so bad.

"That's what broke y'all up—The Funshiners—wasn't it? Tyrane wasn't the only Funshiner whose heart went pittipat at that picnic. Yours did, too."

"We don't need to talk about this now, Eldy, damn it!" he yelled at me.

"We do too! Y'all got in a fight over it, and you never forgave Tyrane for gettin' Leona LeSeur. Then she died, and poor Tyrane was so busted up over it, he fell apart."

I could feel myself gettin' madder by the second.

"You were already gone, weren't ya? You ran out on Tyrane. You left him before Leona died, didn't ya? That's what happened."

My voice was rising, but I couldn't help it.

"He didn't have nobody! Were the Funshiners gone too? They were, weren't they?

What he loved most was gone. His best friend picked up his marbles and quit, and the cause of it all is dead! God, that must've hurt. You let your best friend go to hell in a hand basket and didn't do a damn thing to help him! How could you do that?"

I was shouting now, and crying.

"Stop the truck! Stop this damn truck!"

"Eldy, wait a minute. It wasn't like that."

"It was! You walked out on him."

"No! Well, yes, but ..."

"Let me out of this truck. Stop it now!"

I was so damn mad I couldn't hardly see, nor think neither. I pulled up on the door handle. We were goin' over seventy miles an hour. The door released, but the wind was too strong for me to push it open. I was so mad I didn't give no thought to the splat on the highway I'd be if Felton hadn't grabbed my shirt.

"Eldy!"

He dragged me back from the door and pulled onto the shoulder of the highway. When the Studebaker came to a stop, I jumped out yelling insults. I hardly noticed the cool, slick rain cascade down my face. Vaguely, I heard Whistler whining from under the toolbox.

Felton came around the truck and tried to gather me in his arms, but I jerked away and yelled, "Get away from me, you—you damn traitor. Damn you! I never want to see you again. Leave me alone!"

Whistler started barking frantic, the way he does when a coon is tryin' to get in the chicken house.

Felton had to shout above the noise of cars goin' by on the wet pavement and Whistler's carryin' on. Didn't neither one of us pay no 'tention to the spray of the big trucks.

He hollered, "Eldy, it wasn't like that. I left, but I didn't run out on him, not like you're sayin'."

Tractor-trailers roared by, cars and smaller trucks sped past us, even campers with cars attached to their rear lumbered by, and yet the busy interstate highway felt as lonely as badlands in a western movie.

"I can't leave you out here like this, Eldy." He went on pleading. "Get back in the truck. Please."

"I won't. You're just like those people at the house, only you threw him away a long time ago."

I started walking along the highway away from the truck.

Felton ran to me, then grabbed and held me. He shouted, "I didn't know! I would have helped him, Eldy, but I didn't know! That's why I came now! Listen to me!"

Maybe it was the cool rain, Whistler's barking, or, dadgum it, I don't know, maybe I just grew up some right then and there in the rain on the cold war highway. Whatever it was made me listen, and I knew that I wasn't being fair. I stopped, turned, and stared at him.

"That's why I came now," he said again, pleading.

In the rain, Felton's agonized face all twisted up looked like rocks in a clear flowing stream, and suddenly I was ashamed. I felt awful for accusing a man of something bad when I knew so little, and when I had no right to condemn him in the first place. I remembered when I was sent to the office because "Fat Stuff" hit Miss Hurlbutte in the ear with a spitball. It hurt me more that somebody believed something bad about me than the punishment did.

Above the roaring engines and shishing tires of the traffic, Felton hollered, "Get back in the truck, Eldy, please. Let me tell you what happened. It wasn't like what you said. It wasn't."

We got back in the truck and at the next exit, Felton steered the Studebaker into the parking lot of a Waffle House.

"Let's get some coffee, Eldy. I should have told you all of this before now, but I ain't proud of it and I just didn't think it mattered any more."

I was as much a coffee drinker as most grown-ups. Peepee says it's 'cause I'm just trying to act like a big shot or something like that, but that's not it. I really do like coffee with cream and one and a half sugars. Apple pie and coffee improved our mood, and after we had a few minutes to settle down, Felton told his story.

"We didn't part enemies, Eldridge. We parted as hurt friends, ya might say. You were right about Leona. She captured my heart, too. She didn't mean to, you understand, 'cause her eyes were only for Tyrane, but she was always nice to everybody."

He told me they met Leona at the picnic where the Funshiners were playing, and they became as tight as brothers and sister.

"Under that, though," Felton said, "there was a burning love that me and Tyrane had for Leona. It came up big-time when Leona's father began trying to break us up. He didn't want his daughter running with musicians. Acidheads and deadbeats is what he called us.

"I didn't want Ty to go after the old man and Leona's brother. He was that upset," he explained. "Edwin Jr. was as big an asshole as Edwin was. I loved Leona, but I knew she loved Tyrane one way, and loved me more like a brother. It almost killed me, but Ty was my best friend, so I stepped aside, not wanting to cause him any more problems than he already had.

"I thought if I talked with Edwin LeSeur, you know one on one, man to man, I could defuse the situation. On the other hand, I knew Ty wouldn't want me to intercede on his behalf. In those days, Tyrane Percival was a proud man, so I thought if I could get LeSeur to back off without him knowing, I would be helping the two people I loved most in the world in the only way I could.

"But it backfired. I told LeSeur they really were in love, that Ty was a good man, which he was, and that he ought to back off, 'give 'em a chance,' I told him. Edwin Jr. was there too. First thing I knew, Leona's brother told Tyrane that I went behind his back telling the old man to keep his daughter away from Tyrane Percival.

"Ty confronted me about it all upset. I guess deep down I hoped the old man would succeed, and I would get Leona or some such stupidity. Anyway, like a damn fool, instead of calmly explaining what had transpired, I got mad. Pride, you know. We yelled at each other. Tyrane said I didn't care about him or Leona, and I lost it, hit him full in the mouth. Leona was a mess of tears, seeing two best friends goin' at it like worst enemies. It was awful. We were both so damn stupid."

He took a bite of pie, the look of pain in his eyes told me he was wishing then was now, and that he could take it all back. Felton said that he stayed with the band a few more weeks, he and Tyrane not speaking.

"We didn't stay mad, but the rift was like a chasm. Tyrane tried to get me to stay, but I finally quit the band," he said sadly.

"I got the hell out of New Iberia, took up with a touring religious band, and tried to forget those blue eyes and a man I would have killed for. I tried like hell to drown the memory of Leona and my best friend, Tyrane Percival, in booze and marijuana. I woke up one day, penniless, and discovered years had passed, my banjo and guitar were gone—where, I had no idea—and I hardly knew who the hell I was. I did rodeos—I was a pretty good bull rider. Played some gigs with a borrowed banjo, even wrote for a newspaper for a few years."

He explained that he met and married Linda, "a pretty woman and a good person who deserved better." They settled in Minnesota. He got a job at a big dairy, Jeff was born, and everything was going along all right, even though he was still drinking way too much.

"A few years ago I got a letter from New Iberia. I don't know how they found me way the hell up there, but they did. One of the band members wrote me a letter. By the postmark, it took a long time to find me, and might not have at all, if I hadn't left forwarding addresses everywhere I went. I think I did that hoping that someday I would hear from Tyrane or some of the Funshiners.

"But what I heard from them sent me into a tailspin. Don't get me wrong, I loved Linda and Jeff, but learning that my first love, Leona LeSeur, was dead, and Tyrane had gone to jail and disappeared, just tore me up like I didn't think anything could. I was already drinkin' too much, and, well, you can imagine what happened.

"One Friday night, I passed out in this same truck near the dairy.

That's where they found me to tell me the bus Linda and my eight-year-old son Jeff were in went off a bridge.

"I quit drinking, and vowed I was gonna get my life back together, and I've been doing that ever since. I knew I could never do it without telling Ty I was sorry for not being there when he and Leona needed me, and trying to make him understand why I left so abruptly. I owed him that."

The whole time Felton was talking, I was thinking about how much it hurt losin' Daddy, and how much better it felt now. I know I ain't grown up, just a shave tail kid and all, but I think I knew what he meant, what was eatin' at him.

"I'm sorry, Felton. I didn't mean all those awful things I said. I was just ..."

I wanted to make him feel better the way he done for me by the pool.

He smiled and went on as though I hadn't spoken.

"I had some rehab, Eldy. Hell, I had a lot of it. Anyway, then I started tracking him down. Finally, a fella I knew called and told me where Tyrane was. I left the next day for Jupiter Bluff with your Aunt's address in my pocket. When I got to your Aunt Bessie's and saw the way you was runnin' to your Mama's, I knew something terrible had happened. When I went into your Mama's living room, I had already been to your Aunt's house. I found him the same way you did, with his fiddle in his lap and vacant eyes. I didn't know about you or your mama until they told me who you were."

Felton got a little choked up and had to stop for a few seconds. He waved for a refill of his coffee.

It was weird. I wasn't cryin' but I felt a tear slide down my cheek anyway.

"He looked so peaceful in that old rocking chair with his fiddle in his lap. I sat there with him for quite a while. It was hard seeing him like that, after all those years of playing gigs with him, laughing together in the bus on tour, playin' poker in the back. He was the finest man I ever knew, Eldy. I'm gonna miss him more now than I did all those years we were apart."

During the long ride from home, Felton told me many stories about Tyrane and the Funshiners. "Anecdotes" is what he called 'em. He told me this one over coffee at the Waffle House.

One day their tour bus broke down out in the country. It was hot as blazes, so he and Ty hiked to a farmhouse to get water, while their piano player, who was a jackleg mechanic, worked on the bus. The farmhouse was rundown with a sagging gate, weed-grown yard, and house in need of paint.

Felton said it was a scene like was in The Grapes of Wrath, which I think is a old black and white movie he saw one time. There were three little kids runnin' around in rags. A young widow lady sat on the porch steps looking like there wasn't nothin' left, and that she couldn't go on.

The lady looked a lot older, but they were sure she was no more than thirty years old. Her husband had been killed in an accident, and her money had run out. She used their last dollar for the veterinarian to treat their milk cow. Without their tractor and with no money left, saving the farm would be impossible, and the finance company was coming to get the machine.

While Tyrane and Felton were sitting there on the steps with her, a big Cadillac drove up in the yard. The driver was a big pig in an expensive pea green suit and yellow tie, and he was pompous as an angry blue jay. He nodded toward a tractor that had to be more than ten years old, and said to the man with him, a big mean-looking country fella wearing overalls and a glistening layer of sour sweat, "That's it yonder."

Apparently, the big guy was going to drive the tractor, because he demanded that the lady give him the keys to it. Blue jay announced when he got to the steps, "We're gonna have to take the tractor, Mrs. Priester. You done had enough time. I told you that this morning."

Tyrane stepped up, smiled politely, and said, "Now just hold on a minute there, Mister. I'm sure we can work something—"

The blue jay interrupted rudely. "There ain't nothin' further to talk about workin' out. And who the hell might you be, mister, to butt in to what ain't none of your business?"

Tyrane's face went still like a graveyard at midnight, and then he said, "Friend, I don't hold with bad manners and I'll ask that you try to be civil. I'm the fella that just told you to hold on a minute! I meant it, too. Now, why don't you calm down and let's me and you discuss this thing, and maybe come to an arrangement."

The big country boy hooked his thumbs in the straps of his denim bib overalls. He reared back with his chin stuck out and said to Tyrane angrily, "You just butt out! This here ain't none of y'all's business. This woman ain't paid nothin' on our tractor in months, and we done come to take it back. You'd do well to stay the hell out of what ain't none of your business."

Felton had bit off a plug of tobacco and was chewing it hard—getting it ready. As he casually pointed across the yard, he put a hand, easy like, on the country boy's huge forearm and asked, "Look here, mister, are you the one gonna drive that old rusty tractor yonder for this—" Felton paused for a frank appraisal of the blue jay—"fancy fop that looks like a unripe okra pod?"

Surprised that someone so much smaller would interrupt him, the country boy turned to Felton. For a second, he hesitated as if bothered by a fly, then balled his fist and answered with a snarl, "Yeah, that's what I'm gonna do. You got a problem with that? What's it to you?"

"To me?" Felton asked, wide-eyed as if he couldn't believe the guy asked such a question. "Hell, man, it's nothin' to me. It means a lot to you, though. I sure hope he's payin' you a whole lot of money to do it."

"What the hell are you talkin' about, asshole?"

"What I'm talkin' about is, if you go near that tractor, I'm gonna rip your damn head off!"

The country boy cursed and come at Felton, which was a big mistake.

He got a face full of tobacco juice, followed by knuckles on the point of his jaw, and he went down like a felled steer. He lay on the ground, out cold, his face covered by brown ooze running slowly down his cheeks.

The blue jay stared dumbstruck at how easily his muscle had been bested. His face drained of color and his lips trembled. He stared down at the prone denim-clad figure on the ground, then at Felton, who casually spat on the ground at his feet, and then at Tyrane who was smiling.

Tyrane asked, "You didn't kill him, did'ya?"

Felton shook his head and said, "Naw, sometimes when I hit 'em like that, the jaw bone snaps and goes up into the brain. I didn't hit him that hard."

Felton hesitated, looked down at the figure on the ground, kicked his shoe and added with a grin, "Or at least, I don't think so."

Tyrane turned to the blue jay and said, "Now that you understand how we feel about this matter, maybe we can talk about it. How much does she owe on the tractor, Mister?"

With hands trembling, the blue jay fumbled in his coat pocket and produced a piece of paper which fluttered as if a strong wind was blowing, although there was no breeze whatsoever.

He mumbled, "It's … It's all … here."

Ty accepted the paper, studied it a while, nodded and said, "Friend, the way it looks to me, this little lady has paid for that tractor at least twice since her husband bought it four years ago. Since you've been gouging her shamelessly the whole time, I believe it would be only fair if she gives you one more payment, and then the debt would be paid in full."

Tyrane turned to Felton with a grin. "What do you think, Banjo?"

Felton rubbed his chin and nodded. "Sounds fair to me, Ty. How about you. ma'am? You think that there is a fair compromise, one more payment, and the tractor is yours free and clear?"

The woman all this time had stood spellbound by the exchange. She muttered, "Well, I just ... I don't know. I ... I guess so." She wrung her hands against her breast.

A little blonde girl in shabby clothes clung to her faded dress.

I interrupted Felton's story to ask, "He called you Banjo, Felton? Is that what they called you back then?"

He ignored my question and described how Tyrane counted out forty-three dollars from his wallet, groped around in his pocket for eighteen cents in change and stuffed the money in the handkerchief pocket of blue jay's suit. Then he grabbed him by the collar and the seat of his pants and propelled him to his car. Pointing at the hood, he said, "You can use that as a desk while you write on that invoice, paid in full. Do it now."

Felton said the man was a comical sight, stretching down to write on the paper while being held at a slant over his car's hood. When he finished, Tyrane released him, leaned in close to his face and warned coldly, "If you or that piece of crap ever come around here or bother this lady and her family again, I'll come back and make you eat that tractor, one tire at a time. You got that, you son of a bitch?"

When last seen, the blue jay and his tractor driver were getting out of there as fast as the Cadillac could master the dirt road.

The Funshiners had dinner with the woman and her children, left her some extra money, and went on their way.

"I didn't know until one of the band members told me that Tyrane sent money to that woman and her family for months until they could get on their feet."

"Felton?"

"Yeah, Eldy."

"How come you don't play the banjo anymore? Your hands ain't hurt."

He looked away and this time I knew it was a tear gathering in the bottom of his eye.

"A very long time ago, I promised myself I wouldn't play again until I could stand beside Tyrane and play for him and Leona."

It was nigh onto three o'clock when we finally got to New Iberia, Louisiana, and Felton attempted to find his way around a town he said was nothing like he remembered it. We went down some one-way streets the wrong way, got screwed up in some kind of circles that Felton called cul-de-sacs, and had to retrace our path a few times, but eventually we found the place Felton was looking for.

Sol's Fine Clothes was still in business, although it had moved to a major shopping center, north of town called North Town Shopping Center. I come to think that they ain't real original when it come to names in New Iberia.

Felton explained that the store being moved was why it took him so long to find it. "It was in the historic district when I was here," he said.

I thought, yeah, and my back porch in West Virginia, has a great view of the beaches of the Atlantic Ocean. I didn't say it, but he saw it in my face because he snorted.

"Well it was twenty years ago, you know. Damn!"

We parked the truck kind of away from the other cars, told Whistler he was "on duty," and went into the store.

When I walked into that place, I near about dropped my britches at what I saw. I stared the way I did in church when that mouse run up Sister Camellia's leg and she tore off her choir robe and dress. Lot of folks thought I had something to do with that, but I swear that it wasn't me. I wish I'd thought of it though.

I couldn't believe the clothes on racks all over the place and the strange people in the store trying them on. I didn't know they made men's suits as bright red as Santa Claus's, canary yellow suits that hung almost to the knees, or shiny blue suits that looked like sparking electricity.

Two young freaky-looking guys were posing for each other in front of a full-length mirror. I wasn't real sure which they were, boy or girl, a something another in between. They modeled silk shirts of crimson and bright green.

I thought, I'd kill to show this to old Peepee. He'll swear on his Mama's chop suey that I'm lying when I tell him about this stuff. The two men, or women—or whatever—had decorated themselves with enough of these tiny metal rings to sink a battle ship. They had seven or eight little silver loops around the edges of their ears and three or four tiny rings in their eyebrows and, I swear if I'm lyin' I'm dyin', one had a pearl on each side of his nose. One of them had hair that was bright violet like the flowers! The other one had hair that was—I swear I'm not making this up—green and yellow stripes.

Standing off from the rest of the store, looking like a dying prospector in the desert, was a real tall, bony old man in a gray suit. He had absolutely no hair at all—I mean none at all—eyebrows included. From the neck up, he was tight skin over skull, and nary a hair of any kind. He seemed out of place, but acted as if he belonged.

I think that's what you call a paradox. Miss Hurlbutte would've give me a 'A' for remembering that one.

Chapter Ten

I ain't never seen nothin' like that place, but Felton didn't seem at all surprised at any of it. I think it was what he expected. He led the way to a busy round sales counter in the center of the store where a woman and two men were trying to get out of each other's way in the space in the center. The woman was black, no more than four and a half feet tall, and despite the chaos around her, in complete control.

She dismissed a customer with a wave and said, "Break a leg."

I wondered why she told the customer that, since I didn't hear him say anything bad to her. But, holy macaroni, maybe in this weird place it made sense. Her dark eyes flickered curiously at Felton's bearded face with what might have been recognition, but I thought that was hardly possible.

"What can we help with, you?" she said in a funny way of talking that Felton told me later was Cajun.

"Is that some kind of different language, Felton? I thought we was still in America." I asked him.

"Well we are, Eldy. I think it's a mishmash of French and English." He explained.

"Oh. You mean something like me and Peepee talk pigeon English?"

"Not exactly, but …"

Felton said to the clerk, "We need to buy a suit for a friend. We ain't exactly sure of his size, ya know, but he got clothes from here before, and I thought y'all might be able to help us."

The woman grabbed the arm of one of the men in the tight little hole.

"Get out from behind the counter, you. You in the way anyway. Help two out-of-towners buy a suit for a friend. Go along now, you."

The man sidled past the others and came through a narrow opening in the circular counter. He looked like Punky's plastic Ken doll, pink-faced, stiff and spit-polished neat as a cadet on a parade ground.

"My name is Albert, sir, and it would be a pleasure to help you. What did you have in mind for your friend?" Then he added, "Don't let the gaudy things confuse you, sir. We have fine traditional suits as well as these, uh, showy things. These are, well, you know I'm sure."

Felton turned to me and said, "I'm thinking of a white suit, Eldridge. What do you think?"

He seemed like he really wanted my opinion, which made me feel good.

"The suit he had had pin stripes and was dark gray wasn't it, Felton? Shouldn't we get one, you know, like you're supposed to wear to church or a wedding or something or other like that?" Then I thought for a minute. "Mama and Aunt Bessie might get all riled up mad if we don't do this right."

"Yeah, I know, and I'd say you were right, except the best time of Tyrane's life was when he was playin' with me and the Funshiners."

He hesitated a second, looked as if he was back in time again, and then went on. "He was wearing a white suit when we played that picnic and saw Leona for the first time, blue eyes just a shinin' up at him."

"I take it that you gentlemen are musicians and your friend is, too? Interrupted Albert, "I somehow thought—"

Felton held up a hand. "Just hold your marbles there, Albert. This is probably the most important thing about a funeral. The dearly departed has to be properly attired when he's trying to talk his way into the gate. The Gatekeeper is persnickety about stuff like that."

He turned back to me. "Besides, Leona might be extra pleased if he was to come to her in his white suit."

"White it ought to be!" I said without hesitation or reservation. "Yes sir, white!"

Albert raised an eyebrow and his mouth turned down as he said, "If the gentleman is going to a funeral, he should wear black, I think, or perhaps something dark at least. I don't think white is the appropriate color for a funeral." He laughed. "Unless it is for the dearly departed, which is still a bit unusual, but there could be reasons, I suppose."

"You got it, Albert. We need a white suit. Our friend has to look like a white turtle dove at this funeral."

Albert rolled his eyes.

"If you will walk this way," he said, "I'll show you something in white."

He turned and led us to a rack of suits.

I chuckled and told Felton, "I can't walk that way, Felton. My butt would go out of joint. He walks like a girl. He saaashades."

Felton smothered a laugh and said, "Just follow Albert, all right?"

Albert asked over his shoulder, "What is the gentleman's size, sir?"

Felton shook his head. "I don't know, Albert. He stands about, oh, maybe this here tall (he held his palm down just above his own shoulders) and he's built about like the boy there, only lots taller."

"Sir, I'm not sure I know what that means, uh, in a size, you know. You don't know his actual size? Even his weight would help."

"Well, I don't know about his weight. He was sitting down and already gone when I got there. How about that, Eldy, you got any idea how much Tyrane weighs?"

"No I don't. He weighed more than me but less than Aunt Bessie. 'Course everybody weighs less than Aunt Bessie."

"I wear a 36 long, I think, but Tyrane is bigger than me. Or at least he used to be." Felton said thoughtfully. He brightened. "Let me ask you something, Albert. Are you good at guessing sizes by looking at the customer? A lot of you fellas that sell suits are good at that. Are you?"

That struck a nerve in old Albert. He smiled at Felton smugly. He held his head up like a butler, chin pointing at a light fixture overhead and said promptly, "I am the best, sir. The best! Where is your friend if you wish me to make such a guess? Why don't you just bring him in and I can take the proper measurements?"

Felton thought a minute and then said, "Well, we can do that, but you got to promise not to go ballistic when you see him."

"Sir, I have been selling men's suits for quite a while, almost four years, and I'm sure I can control my emotions. Thank you very much." Albert looked at Felton like somebody does when your deodorant quits on you in a crowded elevator. "Bring your friend in, sir. I'm sure I can fit him properly."

Felton rubbed his hands together in anticipation, and warned, "Okay, if you promise not to go nuts when you see him."

Albert rolled his eyes again.

Felton motioned to me. "C'mon, Eldy, let's go get Tyrane so Albert here can take some measurements. We want that suit to fit him right. Leona would be disappointed if it didn't."

It took a few minutes to dry off the plastic so it wouldn't soak Felton when he shouldered Tyrane, which he did with surprisingly little effort. We had stopped earlier to refill the ice. Whistler acted downright upset at us taking his master out of the kiddy pool. He gave Felton a good whistle to demonstrate his unhappiness at the turn of events.

Felton said, "Damn if they ain't the awfullest I ever smelt when Whistler puts his mind to it."

I don't know if I got the words to describe poor old Albert's reaction when Felton laid Tyrane, wrapped in Saran Wrap, and urged Albert, "We'll have to hurry this up, Albert, on account he can't stay out of his kiddy pool too long. See, Albert, he's bigger than me. His shoulders and all is wider. Don't you think so, Eldridge?"

I was surprised and a little scared at Albert's reaction and the way everybody in the store gathered round us. With his attention on Tyrane, Felton didn't see what was happening with the clerk.

Albert's eyes plumb jumped out of his head, and his mouth flopped open and shut—blap blap blap—like those false teeth novelties me and Peepee used to buy at the fair. He fell back against the counter, and slid down onto the floor like melting jello.

"Oh Lordy, Eldy," Felton said in alarm. "We done shocked the poor man into oblivion."

He slapped Albert's blanched face, not too hard, but smartly, snatched off the porkpie hat and vigorously fanned the clerk's face, now all shiny with perspiration.

"Oh, my God! Oh, my God!"

Albert said it over and over, each one squeakier than the last, until he sounded like a mouse. He wiped his face with a handkerchief as his eyes began to focus on the bearded, concerned face in front of him.

I tried to help calm the poor fella down.

"It's all right, Mister Albert. There ain't no call to be upset. He's dead. That there is Tyrane Percival on the floor. That's why we brought him all the way from Jupiter Bluff, West Virginny. Not cause he's dead. Well, that too, of course," I said enthusiastically, thinking that my explanation, me bein' a boy 'n all, might help ease the poor man's nerves.

"If he wasn't dead, we wouldn't have brought him down here. See, here's what happened. The moths 'bout ate him up, not him, I mean his old suit which he didn't much wear anyway, and that's why come we have to get him a new one to be buried in. We didn't know the moths ate it 'til last night at the Dew Drop Inn in Alabama. Besides which, the suit he had wasn't right for him to lie by his true love. We're gonna bury him right here in Louisiana beside Leona."

The folks gathered around were buzzing with excitement and crowded close in on us. Albert's voice was as squeaky as the door to our basement. He said, "M–m–m moths? Bury him? Oh my God! W–what's J–Jupiter Bluff?"

Felton straightened up, moved back and commanded forcefully, "Now y'all back up. Give the poor man some air. C'mon, can't y'all see he's been stricken with apoplexy and is struggling to git his breath?"

To tell the truth, I wasn't sure poor Albert would ever be the same. Either the sight of a dead man wrapped in painter's plastic, or of me and Felton acting as if we haul dead men around all the time, was just too much for poor Albert. There ain't no telling what might have happened next if the old baldheaded guy hadn't come to investigate all the commotion.

The old man stared for several minutes at Felton and I could tell that he was trying to see through the beard. He began to smile, "Banjo Haliday! As I live and breathe, Banjo Haliday come back from the dead!"

Felton stopped fanning the ashen face of poor Albert with his hat and turned around to see who was speaking to him. I think he couldn't believe his eyes, because for a moment, he was plain jaw-droppin' speechless. Then he smiled and extended his hand.

"How are you, Sol? It's been a long time."

It turns out the old man was Sol Goldstein, the owner of Sol's Fine Clothes, and he smiled warmly as he gripped Felton's hand and said like he just got his first bicycle, "It's good to see you, Banjo. I ... we gave up ever seeing you again. Where did you go? What happened? Are you still playing anywhere?"

He held Felton back from him a moment to study him as if to measure him for the suit.

"Let me look at you. How long, Banjo? Fifteen years? More?" He shook his head. "You look well, but the miles, they really show up, old friend."

Felton laughed. "They were hard miles, Sol. Almost twenty years of 'em since I seen you last." He glanced at me. "I'm trying to go back over some of them to make sure I touch third base, you know?"

"I heard stuff, Banjo. We lost track of The Fiddle Man and most of the Funshiners a few years after you left. I heard some discouraging things about Tyrane years ago, and then there was nothing."

I don't think Goldstein noticed what was on the floor, because he was so happy to see Felton Haliday. He put a hand on Felton's shoulder.

"Come back to my office, and tell me what's going on in your life. Do you know where Tyrane is now, or how he's doing? Who's this young man? Not your son, I know, because I heard ... I mean ... Oh God, Banjo, I'm sorry."

Felton smiled and said gently, "It's all right, Sol. This is Eldridge Brewer, a friend of mine. We came all the way from a little town in West Virginia."

He stepped back so Sol could see the figure on the floor in its plastic shroud and went on in a tight voice.

"I found Tyrane, Sol, but I was too late, too late by an hour or so. He's here with me and Eldy, though. You see, Sol, that's what we're doing here. We came to buy 'The Fiddle Man' a suit to be buried in, so that when he confronts Heaven's Gatekeeper, he'll look his best, and because we're taking him to be buried next to Leona."

If Solomon Goldstein was shocked, or even surprised for that matter, that a customer brought a dead body into his store to be measured for a new suit, or that it was an old friend, he never let on. Over the course of the next few days, I learned that Sol Goldstein had been around musicians and show people for so long he was used to the crazy things they do.

The people who had gathered got so quiet you could've heard a soap bubble pop. I wondered whether they were thinkin' about their own self, lyin' dead on the floor of a men's store, and about who would care so much to stand over them like me and Felton were.

Boy, I wished Mama was there.

Sol Goldstein stared down at Tyrane Percival for a couple of beats and then slowly knelt beside him. His old bones crackled like corn popping. Sol placed a hand on his heart. Not bothered by the ice chips clinging to the plastic, or paint drops that survived the rain, the old man gently patted Tyrane's head.

He said reverently, "Oh Fiddle Man, I'm so sorry. God go with you, Fiddle Man. God go with you."

He stayed squatted by Tyrane at least a minute longer, rose with a great sigh, and turned to Albert who was coming back from never-never land.

"Albert, give me your measuring tape," he said, "and you go on in the back and get some water, take a break. We'll take care of this."

Albert looked like one of my T-shirts in a washing machine, agitated enough to wrinkle every square inch, and then dumped out. He muttered like he was sure about nothing.

"But, Mr. Goldstein, that's a dead man, sir. Shouldn't we call somebody, the police, or 911? I mean, we can't just, uh … They wanted me to measure him, sir. I couldn't do, I mean …"

Albert's voice got more desperate but it only made it that much squeakier and I thought he might actually cry.

"I can't measure a dead man, Mr. Goldstein!"

As though soothing a child with a stubbed toe, Sol patted his shoulder and said, "I know, Albert. I know. Go on now. I'll take care of this. Everything's going to be all right."

Sol and Ruby Begonia, the black lady from the service counter, measured Tyrane and helped us put him back in the kiddy pool then the four of us settled into Sol's back office. The black lady was real sad, and it seemed to me more than about somebody that she only knew a little. Felton had to translate her Cajun way of talking for me.

The old man must have known everybody in the music business for the last fifty years. Most of the names I heard didn't mean anything, but others were famous, like Elvis Presley, Pat Boone, and Louis Armstrong.

Felton told them what happened to the Funshiners and how he

ended up in Minnesota, then set out to find Tyrane. He told them how it came to be that we brought Tyrane to New Iberia to be buried next to Leona LeSeur and the trials we had getting there.

"If it hadn't been for young Eldridge here," Felton said, "I think we'd still be in Alabama. Somebody didn't want us coming here and the only person I can think of that would want to stop us is Leona's brother, Edwin Jr. He hated Tyrane."

I tried not to let too much get said 'fore I stuck my nose in. I piped up, "My Uncle Felix probably called him on account when he left the house he was still picking mayonnaise out of his hair."

Sol look puzzled. "Mayonnaise in his hair?"

I couldn't keep from laughing a little as I explained. "I threw my ham sandwich and got him square betwixt the eyes, when he started running his mouth about Tyrane bein' a jailbird."

Felton shook his head and held up a hand in disapproval.

"Now, Eldy, that's not something you should be proud of. You were upset, which kind of excuses such bad behavior, but it ain't right to gloat over it."

"I ain't gloatin', Felton, but he's a flyin' asshole and dadgum sure had it comin' right enough. Knowin' he ratted on us and probably got the biker gang for LeSeur, I wish now I'd hit him in the nuts with one of my fast balls."

Sol chuckled. "Sounds like young Eldridge here would make a fine Funshiner, Banjo. I can recall some things I heard about when you went on tour, like ..." he paused, remembering, "... like the advance man of the Grand Ole Opry trying to swim across a mud puddle in Memphis."

Getting back to what we were talking about, namely the LeSeurs, Sol said he got along well with the senior LeSeur, but his son was another matter.

"Edwin Jr. is nothing like his father, Banjo. He's a member of the club I belong to, and not a very popular one. Nobody blackballed him when he joined, in deference to his father, who was alive then. The old man was wrong and misguided when it came to Tyrane and his daughter, but he wasn't the no-good son of a bitch Junior is."

Felton nodded and replied, "I always felt the old man was a decent guy. The letter he wrote to Tyrane confirms it." He paused a moment and then added, "at least in the end."

Felton stood up. "Sol, I wish we could stay longer, but we got to get Tyrane to the funeral home so he can get dressed up for the send-off. When it's all over, me 'n Eldy will come back and spend some time with y'all."

Sol stood too. "What are you going to do, Banjo?"

"Well, Tyrane Percival was the best friend I ever had, Sol. I let him down once. I won't do it again. Me and Eldy are gonna bury him next to Leona LeSeur, like I believe he would want. Edwin LeSeur Sr. said he was saving the burial plot next to Leona for him. I got his letter in my pocket. I figure I'm gonna need it when we get to Ichthius Tweedleman."

"What's a ... Ichthius Tweedleman?" I wanted to know if it might've been some kind of rash you get in your privates.

Felton chuckled. "He's the undertaker. He's still there at the Not Forgotten Funeral Home, ain't he Sol?"

"Ichthius Tweedleman!" I said, laughing. "With a name like that, Sounds like he's already been under took." They ignored me, although I don't know how. Peepee would've fell off the tree limb in the backyard laughing his head off.

Sol Goldstein rubbed his hairless chin thoughtfully. "Yeah, he's still going strong, just like me. You wouldn't mind if I let a few friends know about Tyrane would you, Banjo? Maybe tell 'em when the funeral's gonna be?"

Felton smiled. "I don't see any harm in that, Sol. In fact, that'd be mighty kind of you. I need to settle up with you for the suit and other stuff. What do I owe you for Tyrane's suit and Eldy's Bayou Teche cap and T shirt?"

Sol smiled. "Banjo, it would be an honor for me if The Fiddle Man met Leona in one of my white suits. As far as the other stuff is concerned, it seems to me I can pay tribute to Tyrane Percival by presenting it to his protégé. Do you mind?"

Felton smiled and nodded solemnly. "I'm sure Tyrane and Leona appreciate it, Sol."

Later on Felton told me Sol Goldstein's reputation as a miser was legendary and for him to do this was so unheard of, Felton was scared a refusal would be an insult.

My face burned. Who in the flying fool did he think he was, calling me a protojay?

"I ain't no damn proto... protojay!" I said hotly. "I got my own money Mama gave me when we left out of Jupiter Bluff. We ain't exactly rich, but we don't need nobody's handouts. I ain't no kind of jay."

Sol laughed. "Young man, it's no wonder The Fiddle Man took to you. You're something else. Don't worry, it's not a handout. That's not an insult, son. It's recognition of a man's value by his elders. A protégé is a youngster that a man has taken to his heart in friendship and honor as Tyrane has you. Banjo says he taught you to play the fiddle. That makes you his protégé. I'm genuinely proud to know you, sir."

I didn't really know what to say to that. I still wasn't sure about it, but at least I knew the cap and T shirt weren't handouts and that Sol was saying good things about me. I looked over at Felton and saw the look of satisfaction. Then I noticed that he looked proud. I reckoned it was all right, so I let it go.

Chapter Eleven

We walked across the parking lot toward the truck thinking our own thoughts, Felton probably studyin' about all we had to do to bury Tyrane and me thinking about Peepee and all I had to tell him when I got back to Jupiter Bluff about my adventures driving to Louisiana with Tyrane and Whistler and Felton.

As we got close to the Studebaker, an old Volkswagen bus of many colors lumbered into the opposite side of the parking lot. Slogans of every kind and color were painted on it. As it maneuvered into a parking space, I decided it must have been white first, but with all the slogans and bumper stickers, you couldn't be sure what color it was. A big plastic bumblebee was mounted above the windshield, a stuffed tiger tail hung from the gas tank door, and a pair of red and white striped feet, like those of the Wicked Witch of the West under a house, stuck out of a window. A cloud of heavy smoke belched from the exhaust each time the driver gave it gas to back up or pull forward.

He finally got it in the parking slot, but not before sending a shopping cart rolling toward a grocery store, where it flipped end over end at the curb.

I was so fascinated by the bus and the spray-painted slogans that I couldn't take my eyes off it and walked slap into the side of our truck. Whistler came to the rail for his scratch behind the ears, but he jumped back because of my clumsiness.

I called across to Felton, "Felton, would you look yonder? You ever see anything like that in your whole cotton pickin' life?"

About that time, the bus backfired sending a great mushroom cloud of smoke out of the exhaust as if the damn thing was tellin everybody

"HERE I BE!"

The bus was something to see all right, but the fella who got out was something else again. He was the hugestest Indian ever I seen. He was bigger than John Wayne, bigger than them professional wrestlers you see on TV, bigger even than the jolly green giant! He didn't walk like most folks. He lumbered and kind of rolled—sort of threw his feet out in front just before toppling over.

Glory to a flying wonder, he was coming our way.

Felton was fixing to get in the Studebaker and turned around to see what I was talking about. He stared, frozen, at the wild-looking giant coming toward us. A grin started in his eyes and then spread to the rest of his face until it was pure joyous recognition.

"Chief!" he shouted and literally ran laughing to the big guy and threw his arms around him. The Indian lifted Felton off the ground as if he was no bigger 'n me, hugging him like a baby, brownish red face glowing about like old Peepee when he hit his only homerun, an inside-the-park knock, but you'd have thought he was Mickey Mantle.

The Indian wore buckskin pants and a shirt with the sleeves cut off just below the seam with the fringes flailing wildly. His salt and pepper hair was pulled back into a ponytail with two great eagle feathers in a ring around it, and he wore a headband made of beads. His face was broad, didn't have no whiskers, and knobby as an old stump. He had a hook nose and eyes deep set and dark. His skin was the color of Mama's baked sweet potatoes.

The Indian laughed and said, "Chief never so happy see friend Banjo again! Life good. Bring you back."

"Me too, Chief. Me too!" cried Felton, seemingly unable to stop clapping his hand on the big Indian's shoulder.

"Where you go leave us so long, Banjo? Chief Wampooti miss little banjo man. Funshiners gone. Sad times. Drums not same," the Indian said. "Clothesman Goldstein call Chief. Tell about Tyrane. Chief sad."

I looked around to see if I was dreaming all of this. Maybe this whole business with Tyrane, Whistler and Felton was a flying dream, and I'd wake up and find myself in my teddy PJs in my bed and that there was no trucker, or Brubaker or Crossover, Alabama. I'm dreaming now that I'm in a cowboy movie, I thought, and wondered where the horses and teepees and stagecoaches were.

The Indian was still talking. "Play drums all over with many bands. They try make Chief happy. No good. Make money with drums because Chief best drummer in music tribe, but he not happy. They smoke devil grass and suck white shit up nose. Not like Funshiners. We not need grass and powder to be happy or make music."

Still laughing, Felton untangled himself from the massive arms encircling him. He stepped back and looked up at the big man.

"Chief Wampooti, of the Ho Non Wah clan of Chickasaws, you look wonderful, man."

I was beginning to think Felton had forgotten me, but he turned and gestured to me to come forward. I ain't never been one to hang back, as I guess you done noticed by now, but I did this time. Maybe I was a little afraid because the man was soooo big, or maybe I was a little jealous, too. Who was this guy who Felton Haliday was so happy to see?

Felton pulled me in front of the Indian as if to sacrifice me to King Kong as he announced, "Eldridge Brewer, this here is Chief Wampooti of the Ho Non Wah clan of the Big River Chickasaw, the best skin beater ever to set a rhythm and the drummer of the Funshiners. If he had been around when his cousins did old Custer, the Indians would have won, and me and you would be on reservations."

The huge Indian, suddenly stern, looked down at me as if I was one of his Indian braves and had farted when I bowed to him. Honest to Peepee Phing Phong, it hurt my neck to look up at his face. I even felt my legs tremble a little as Felton went on.

"Chief, may I present the toughest, smartest, bravest kid I've ever known. This here is Eldy. He holds the spirit of music passed along to him by his mentor and benefactor, The Fiddle Man, Tyrane Percival. He can make Ty's fiddle come to life again as if The Fiddle Man was stroking bow on strings."

There was warmth in his gaze, respect, too, I think, but his chiefliness didn't go down none. Chief Wampooti's deep voice rumbled like thunder.

"Little cub too skinny. Need fatten up."

He squeezed my upper arm the way Mama squeezes oranges and went on, "Cub eat too much crap from yellow arches. Squaw cook buffalo for him tonight at lodge. We have festival. Celebrate return of Banjo Man and Fiddle Man. Honor man who carry great music medicine of Fiddle Man after he cross biggest river."

He looked at the truck and the shaggy beast watching him suspiciously. Whistler released a nice e-flat. It crossed my mind that he sometimes farted a warning from the rear end instead of growling from the front.

Chief Wampooti wrinkled his nose. He smiled, thought a minute and went on, "Banjo bring little Fiddle Man and big fart in truck to Chief Wampooti lodge. We cook him, too."

"Hey, hold on there! Now, wait a dadgum minute," I said. "That's Tyrane's dog, Whistler. You can't cook him! Felton!"

Felton laughed and assured me, "The Chief ain't gonna cook the dog, Eldy."

The big Indian laughed which made me think of scraping fingernails on the blackboard.

"Chief make joke, little cub. Not cook big fart. I might stick cork in butt, though."

I tried to laugh about it, but it came out like a sickly snicker.

I said, "Mister Chief, you're just funnin' me, ain't ya? I might not be all growed up, but I didn't just fall off the watermelon truck neither. I know you don't talk like that for real. Nobody talks like that unless they's makin' it up like me and Peepee do in Jupiter Bluff. You ain't really no Indian Chief!"

The huge man's already red face reddened further. He folded his arms and roared as he pounded his massive chest, "I am Chief Wampootiteepa, of Ho Non Wah Tribe! I am full-blood Big River Chickasaw!"

Felton interrupted quickly. "He's a full-blood Indian, Eldy. I think he can talk regular, but if I ever heard him do it, I don't remember it. He swears it ain't put on."

Chief Wampooti gestured us to go with him to his Volkswagen.

"Come Banjo and fiddle man cub, I take to lodge, we smoke pipe, drink firewater, eat buffalo till belly out here."

He held his hands out to demonstrate.

"You tell about Fiddle Man teach you 'Orange Blossom Special.'"

Felton laughed while shaking his head. "Can't do it, oh great Chief. We've got to take Tyrane to Tweedleman at the Not Forgotten Funeral Home to get fixed up for burial. I don't know how long that'll take, but maybe we can get together after."

"Chief go with you. Make sure medicine man not anger spirit of Fiddle Man and make it walk earth pissed off at everything."

Then he turned around and lumbered off toward the colorful "horse" he rode in on. He hollered back, "I follow ancient truck with big fart in back."

Well, I can tell you we was some kind of a sight as we drove through New Iberia, Louisiana. It's a flying miracle that people didn't have no wrecks or something watchin' us go by. Chief Wampooti fell in behind us in the bus which Felton called a "hippie wagon."

The muffler on the bus didn't muffle at all. The fool-lookin' thing roared like the go-karts and funny cars at the Cucumber Cup Championship at Hotrod Harley's dirt track in Jupiter Bluff.

Whistler thought the Chief's VW bus with its bumblebee on top was a monster come to take Tyrane and maybe eat him, and that dog was not gonna let that happen! He planted his self at the tailgate of the pickup and proceeded to give that noisy, smoky-ass thing trailing us unshirted hell, barkin' like the devil done got in his chicken house.

It was no wonder everybody stopped to watch us go by. Here was a rare pea-green antique Studebaker pickup truck driving through downtown New Iberia with a great big old shaggy dog barking so loud you could hear him in every outhouse in Louisiana. And it's followed by a hippie wagon with slogans spray-painted all over it, like We shall overcome, Make love not war, and Don't laugh, your daughter may be in here. It backfired a cloud of blue-black Indian smoke signals in counter rhythm to Whistler's barks.

The funeral home was a great white house on a hill with four big pillars in front. It made me think of those plantations you see in movies and in books at school. It even had a little porch above the main entrance, but you'd have to climb out of a window to get on it, 'cause there was no door.

The driveway curved like a horseshoe in front, which is where Felton drove the pickup and stopped behind a long, black Lincoln Limousine. The hippie wagon fired a shot of black smoke when Chief Wampooti shut off the engine.

A pinch-faced man in the blackest suit I ever did see came down the steps. He looked the way my Aunt Elsie did at the wedding when she saw Cousin Mary Lou smile and a piece of spinach made it seem she didn't have no front teeth.

As he came down the steps chicken clucking, he said in a very disapproving tone, "I beg your pardon, sir, but you will have to move along. You can't park your truck, uh, I mean trucks here. This area is for our clients."

He looked long and hard at the Studebaker and the monstrosity behind it with its engine still burbling as if it had a upset stomach. He thought we were hired to cut grass or something 'cause he said, "The grounds don't need mowing right now. You need not come back. You see we have a commercial firm that does that for us. Please move your, uh, vehicles, right away, if you would."

Felton leaned across me in the passenger seat, waved a hand dismissing the man's concerns and shouted, "It's all right, there, doctor. We ain't yardmen come to trim your hedges or cut the grass. We just gonna unload the dearly departed. After, we'll park around back in case somebody else needs to make the delivery of a dead aunt or uncle."

He shut off the engine, spat out of the window, and turned to me.

"You better take Whistler over to the grassy area yonder and let him do his business. He's been cooped up back there a long time and he needs some exercise. Give him a brisk walk. Me and the Indian will take Tyrane in and get things started."

Felton ignored the distressed man in the black suit, who had apparently attended so many funerals his face was frozen in mourning. As if pallbearers had dropped a casket, he pleaded, "Oh, my goodness! You can't do that! Please, sir. This is highly irregular. You can't …"

About that time, Chief Wampooti came up beside Felton, dwarfing the little funeral attendant whose face turned white while he bravely went on, "… park here. You have to take corpses—bodies—I mean the departed, to the rear."

Chief Wampooti glowered down on the man and said, in that scary rumbling voice, "Fiddle Man is great music chief. Not come in back door like tribal dog."

He slipped his hands under the arms of the speechless attendant, picked him up like a toy soldier, and set him aside where he stood ashen-faced.

"You stay out of way. Not worthy to handle Fiddle Man."

I would have waited to take Whistler so I could see what happened next, but Felton made me go on.

"Can't I come too, Felton?" I asked. "I ain't never done nothin' like this here."

"No Eldy, you look to Whistler." He said firmly and turned back to the truck.

From the grass on the other side of the grounds, I watched Chief Wampooti tenderly lift Tyrane from the ice in the kiddy pool and carry him like a baby up the steps.

The Not Forgotten funeral home fella didn't know whether to crap or go blind as he watched the huge man with eagle feathers flickering in the breeze carry a plastic-wrapped dead man dripping ice cubes up the steps.

Felton followed the Indian up the stairs with his porkpie hat over his heart. At the top, he called across to me in the lawn area, "After Whistler gets his run, Eldy, you come on in. We'll be with Mr. Tweedleman. You can't miss him. He looks like he's been dead since he was born."

Felton waved the hat at the employee who was still standing by the Studebaker with his jaw dropped down in pure awe at what he was seeing.

"Well come on, man. What are you standing there for? Ichthius Tweedleman's got a lot to do to make old Tyrane here acceptable to the Gatekeeper. Close your mouth so the flies don't get in, and come on!"

We had bought a leash for Whistler at a K-Mart, since it didn't seem like a good idea to go to another Mega-Mart. They might have an ASB—that's like a APB only here it means a All Stores Bulletin—out for a man and a greasy boy who was attacked by mad pedalfiles. The leash was in a plastic case, and you pulled it out like a metal tape rule. It was real long and gave old Whistler a lot of room to roam. I tied it off on the branch of a bush and walked back to the plantation house.

The funeral home wasn't nothing like the one in Jupiter Bluff, Harold's Funeral Chapel, Vinyl Siding and Windows Company which I remember well even though I was only in once for Uncle Arthur's funeral after he got threshed by the big red thresher. I guess the Not Forgotten Funeral Home didn't sell nothin', only buried folks. They didn't have stuff displayed like old Mr. Harold did at his Funeral Chapel, Vinyl Siding and Windows Company. At Harold's, they had these little model windows on stands outside of the worshipping chapel. The prices were written on 'em in fancy writing, you know kind of neat and solemn, so's wouldn't nobody get offended 'bout selling stuff at the service.

The grieving men gathered around the display to talk about their own windows, comparing locks, panes, and window frames. It was all kind of homey. Sometimes whilst folks visited the casket, there was a few squeaks and scrapes of them little windows goin' up and down. Didn't nobody seem to mind and it probably made grieving over losing a dear one a little easier, ya know.

Harold's also covered the walls in the chapel with different kinds and colors of vinyl siding. Most people liked that because between bereavements, the widows could think about redoing the house with the insurance money.

The Not Forgotten Funeral Home was like a tomb, graveyard quiet except for an antique grandfather clock in the hall that bonged in my ear, making me 'most jump out of my sneakers. The place had a funny smell, too, that I couldn't pin down. It was like sour peaches and popcorn is the best I could think of. The carpet felt like thick mowed grass, and on the walls were huge pictures of fields and forests.

I came to a glass-fronted door that read Ichthius Tweedleman, III, behind which I could hear voices, including Felton's distinctive scratchy one that arrested everybody in our living room. I could also hear that rumble from the Indian's big chest.

When I opened the door and walked in, I knew right away that we had done stepped into the chicken poop. I could almost feel it oozin' up betwixt my toes.

It was a big fancy office with a black desk as big as Peepee's ping-pong table. Behind it was a man with skin so white he might have been mistaken for a walkin' one of the dearly departeds. His wispy hair was like a white cloud hovering over a pink dome, and his watery blue eyes reminded me of the dead people stumbling around with their arms sticking out in The Night of the Living Dead. Hanging on the wall behind him was a picture of a man who looked exactly like him, except his clothes were from another century: Ichthius Tweedleman, Jr.

Standing at the window looking as if he smelled something rotten was a distinguished-looking fella in a gray suit that I bet cost a million dollars, and a blue and red silk necktie. The expression on his pink face said it all. I knew he must be Edwin LeSeur Jr., and he was there for one reason: to keep us from burying Tyrane Percival next to his sister. I didn't get into the room good before wishing I had a mayonnaisey ham sandwich. I kept my mouth shut though, which as you know by now, ain't easy for me. I sidled over to a chair on the wall behind Felton and Chief Wampooti.

LeSeur's dark eyes were flashing the fire of victory, and his chin stuck out triumphantly.

"So you see gentlemen," he said, "you'll have to bury your jailbird someplace else. I'm certainly not going to stand by while you desecrate the graves of my ancestors with that no good whoremonger, Tyrane Percival."

That did it! I jumped up no sooner than I had sat down, but Felton snapped at me sharp and commanding, "Sit, Eldy!"

And, so I did, but I was mad enough to stomp a butterfly. Instead of a ham sandwich, I wish I had a hand grenade to put up his butt.

Tweedleman said as he shook his head, "The LeSeurs have had that cemetery plot for many generations, Mr. Haliday. I cannot take it upon myself to use it without the family's permission, and since Mister LeSeur here is the only living heir and an appropriate spokesman for the family, I have no choice. Edwin told me he had written to Mr. Percival about the cemetery plot. The letter from the late Mr. LeSeur makes his desires clear, but his son here is legally the executor of his estate and refuses to allow it, which leaves me no alternative.

"However, we'll be glad to prepare Mr. Percival. In fact, I think we should get started on that quite immediately in view of how long it's been since he ... uh ... passed away. With your permission, I'll have my technicians get started."

He picked up a phone and held it ready to dial a number.

Felton looked over at the Chief, who returned his gaze completely without expression.

"Yeah, well that's gotta be done no matter where we plant him. Go ahead with that, Ichthius. We got the suit he's gonna wear hanging up in my truck."

He turned to me, gave me a reassuring smile and said, "Eldridge, run to the truck and get Tyrane's suit and bring it here to Mr. Tweedleman."

I got up, stared daggers at LeSeur and asked, "Is that your Lincoln parked in front of our truck?"

Before he could answer, Felton shook his head and said firmly, "You don't need to do anything with Whistler, Eldy, okay? You just leave him where he's at."

"Aw, Felton ..."

"Eldy!"

"All right, but ..."

"Go on, son. I know how you feel. We'll work it out."

As I was leaving, I heard LeSeur say, "I don't really care where you bury the man, but in deference to my late sister, God rest her sainted soul, I purchased a plot at the new cemetery out in Monroe where you can take him. Tweedleman assures me he can bury him there, and if there's any difference in cost, I'll take care of it."

I hung by the door and heard Felton say, "Edwin, your father was a good man, even if he was a damn fool over Tyrane and Leona. To his everlasting credit, he tried to do what was right at the end. He did the only thing he could to make it up to them both, namely provide for them to be together into eternity. If you can stand there and deny them that, then only God can condemn you in a manner appropriate for such inhuman behavior. And, Edwin, he most certainly will."

When I came in with the suit, LeSeur was walking down the hall to leave. Now, the hall wasn't particularly narrow, but I walked right square down the middle so LeSeur would have to step aside to get by me. There wasn't no way on god's green earth that I was gonna move aside even if the asshole had to slide along the wall to get past! I spread my legs, held my hands in front of me and squatted like when I play fullback. I let the suit hang from a finger.

Me and LeSeur stood staring at one another for a while till he finally snapped disgustedly, "Get out of my way, you little brat," and then reached out to physically move me aside.

Behind him, in that rumbling bass voice like an idling diesel engine and with his lips almost brushing LeSeur's ear, Chief Wampooti said slowly, ominously, "You touch Fiddle Man's shaman cub, Chief Wampootiteepa, Ho Non Wah Tribe of Big River Chickasaw squash you like swamp roach!"

Edwin LeSeur's hand froze within an inch of me and started to tremble. His face drained and turned white as a flying cloud, and then he went around me and hurried out of the building.

The big Indian grinned at me. "White man have too much sense. Not take chance anger big Chief. So much the pity. You come little brave Eldy. Take suit in."

I gave Felton the suit without sayin' anything, but with my most evil eye instead. I was teed off about LeSeur's gettin' in the way, of course, but mostly I was boiling mad that Felton gave in to the smart-ass blowhard without a fight. He was acting like burying Tyrane in some cemetery thirty miles away was all right. Then the damn traitor wouldn't even let me and Whistler give his fancy big car some of Whistler's finest whistles.

Chapter Twelve

When they completed arrangements with the Funeral home, Chief Wampooti invited me to ride in the hippie bus, and I accepted. I knew it surprised Felton, 'cause he raised his eyebrows the way he did when I didn't do what he expected. I didn't care.

My mind was so full of other things that I gave no thought to where we were going. It soon hit me though that this strange giant might actually live in a buffalo hide teepee on some Indian reservation. After all, the way he talked was Indian, wasn't it? Suddenly I could see myself sitting half-naked at a campfire, munching on a buffalo chip. I decided I better find out what this here "lodge" thing was.

"Where do you live, Chief? Is it far?" I had to almost shout to be heard above the engine.

"Lodge not far. Be there soon. Squaw make great feast for cub and banjo man."

"Is your lodge a big one on the, uh, reservation?"

Chief Wampooti gave me a quick glance of surprise.

"How you know Chief live on reservation?"

"I guessed y'all have to, don't you?"

"No! No more!" he snapped. "John Wayne sign treaty, we stay on reservation, but he gone to great movie set in the sky. Can't make us stay on reservation now."

What in the flying fruitcake am I hearing? John Wayne? Chief Wampooti's gnarled face started to wrinkle as he began to laugh, and soon he was laughing his big head off. I felt stupid at first, but soon I was laughing just as hard as he was.

He did live on a reservation as it turned out, but not the kind I was talking about. It was a subdivision named Chickasaw Reservation and had been developed by the Chief himself. His "lodge" was a sprawling ranch house with several acres separating him from the rest of the houses in the subdivision.

His "squaw" was a warm, friendly woman who gathered me in as if I was her long lost child and was now under her personal protection. Her name was Margaret, and although she wasn't big as her, she made me think of Aunt Bessie. 'Course, there ain't nobody big as Aunt Bessie. She had a niceness that just kind of oozed out of every pore in her skin. I liked her right off.

She fussed over me and railed at Chief for not bringing me home sooner. "Tsk tsk," she kept sayin' while she put out milk, cookies and even a wedge of chocolate cake. She was so easy to talk to, I found myself goin' on about my life in Jupiter Bluff and about Mama, Punky and Peepee. She chattered about the Funshiners and about how she used to follow the band everywhere. It wasn't until then that I learned the Chief's official last name. It was Two Cat, but Margaret said he didn't use it much. She said he liked to go through that stuff about the Ho Non Wah Tribe and all that.

I don't know how long we had been talking when it occurred to me that Felton hadn't come in. Alarm bells went to clanging in my head as I recalled those butt-ugly bikers in Crossover, Alabama. I tried to remember when I last looked out the back window of the Chief's hippie wagon. It was only a few minutes after we left the funeral home. There'd been plenty of time. Edwin LeSeur sure as warts on a toad frog wouldn't think twice about gettin' them bikers to jump Felton again.

Chief Wampooti had been in another part of the house most of the time I was with his wife. Now he came into the kitchen and sat down at the table.

"Telephone lines squawking like crazy," he said. "In old days, smoke come on every hill, proclaim arrival of Fiddle Man and Fiddle Man cub."

Real Worried I said, "Chief, Felton ain't got here yet. I thought he was right behind us on the way over from the funeral home. He might've got lost or something or other. Felton told you about them bikers, didn't he? You don't think they would try again, do ya? Not now, anyways. It don't matter none since we done give up on buryin' Tyrane in LeSeur's cemetery plot."

Chief Wampooti looked surprised. He shrugged and said, "Felton all right, Fiddle Cub. He make stops on way to Wampooti lodge. When great fiddlers pass into greatest gig of all, many preparations necessary for spirit to be happy. I, Chief Wampooti, explain to Banjo Man traditional Chickasaw funeral. Do not be alarmed that we have abandoned your purpose. Indians must be cunning when confronting great odds, or stupid generals like Custer."

I was a little relieved that Felton was out arranging for the funeral and not being jumped by the bikers from Alabama. It did seem like the Chief was talking in riddles, though, when it come to where we was gonna bury Tyrane. I asked him what he meant, and got only a crooked grin and a wag of his nose picker.

After a while, I wandered outside to look around. It was my favorite time of the day. There was still plenty of light, the sun caused yellow beams through the trees, and the wind blew cool and easy. It was peaceful and quiet, and even though I was pissed at Felton about Tyrane's burial, I found myself feeling good as when mama nuzzles me, giggling and calling me her "Elde-berry." Even thinking about that made my face red.

The lodge was a big place with as many outbuildings as a West Virginia farm like ours, but it was bigger and in better shape. There were two horses in one of several corrals. I walked over and propped my foot on the bottom fence rail.

I had done some riding on an old horse we once had and at a stable on the other side of town where Daddy used to take me. Outside of striking out Fatstuff from Bickford Street, it was my favorite thing to do.

"Mama said you were cute. I kept waiting for you to come outside so I could find out if you were, but it looked like you were gonna sit at that table 'til your butt took root."

The voice was the sweetest I ever in my life heard. It made me think of that thing mama hung on our front porch with bits of glass and metal on strings that tinkled real pretty when the wind blew it around.

I turned around to see who was calling me cute, which I am of course, only don't many tell me so to my face. When I did, I don't know what happened, but all of a sudden my tongue felt swollen, my breath caught in my throat, and my face caught fire.

I was looking at a girl with shiny black hair, eyes that were the bluest blue and the prettiest little smiley lips in the whole cotton pickin' world. I knew I would never forget them lips if I lived to be a hundred. She had skin the color of a robin's breast.

"Well, aren't you going to say something?"

"Uuuhhh, I ... Hello ... I'm, uh ..."

"Don't you remember your name?"

"No. I mean, yes. It's Eldridge, uh ..."

"Well, Eldridge Uh, are you going to go riding with me or not?"

She wore riding breeches and a shirt tied in a knot in front.

The best I could do was nod like a flying idiot. I must have looked real dumb, standing there tongue-tied, staring at her like a fool. I messed with some of the girls at school, you know, but this was different. She was different. Those girls bugged me with their silly gigglin' and stuff, but this girl; man, her giggles wouldn't bother me at all.

"I'm Sarah Bella Two Cat. Most people call me Bella. What do most people call you?" Her smile almost blinded me.

I couldn't make my tongue work right, like it done come loose from my throat. I just blurted, "You're so pretty. I ..."

"Well, Mama was right, you are cute." Her eyes flashed like them little Christmas twinkle lights. She took my hand in hers and began leading me to the stable. I followed along like a puppy, but I soon got myself straightened around, and tried to hide how I was feeling.

While I was drawing the cinch tight on her saddle, she said, "I heard about your friend and I'm real sorry. You must have liked him a lot to come all the way down here to bury him."

I tried to act like I wasn't goin' nuts lookin' at her and said, "He was teaching me to play the fiddle when he died. He was my best friend, 'ceptin' for Peepee, of course."

"My Daddy used to talk about fiddle man all the time. He said he was a saint." She paused and then asked, "Was that his real name?"

"His name was Tyrane Percival. Oh, you mean Peepee. No. His real name is Phing Phong, but we call him Peepee. He likes it."

"I'd like to meet him."

"You'd like him." I said. Even as I said it, I thought I wouldn't want her to meet him, 'cause she might go to likin' him more 'n me. Here I ain't been with her two full minutes and I was already jealous of any other boy.

We rode the horses all over the neighborhood on trails that weaved all around through it. She was easy to talk to and laughed at all my silly jokes. It was as if we had known each other all of our lives. She said her Daddy, Chief Wampooti, bought the land when it was affordable, and its value had gone through the roof. She said he subdivided it, but insisted on saving as much of its natural beauty as possible.

"Does he always talk funny like some TV Indian?"

Bella smiled sort of mysterious-like, and those blue eyes danced a little jig. "Do you think so?"

"I don't know. Felton said he's never heard him talk any other way."

She laughed gaily, "Well, there you go." She cantered ahead of me and looked back over her shoulder.

God, she was pretty as a speckled pup in a red wagon.

By the time we got back to the stable, I would have traded my skinny butt for a fat one and thrown in my best baseball cards too. I'm a good rider, but I wasn't used to bein' in a saddle that long.

When I got down off that horse, my legs formed a big O and I wasn't sure my knees would ever meet one another again. Not only that, it was all I could do to keep from wobbling when I dismounted.

Bella handed me a brush, and we brushed both horses down after watering, gave each a few sugar lumps and closed their stalls in the stable. I don't know how I missed seeing it earlier, but as we were leaving the stable, I saw the biggest horse I ever saw. Yellow-gray and towering over the other horses, it had a jet-black flowing mane and tail and long hair on its forelegs. In spite of how big it was, it still looked like a racehorse.

Bella said it was a Hanoverian and would only let her father ride him.

"He goes berserk if anybody else gets on him, but he's gentle as a puppy otherwise," she said as she stroked his forehead. The big animal nuzzled her for another sugar morsel, and she gave him one.

Watchin' that horse nuzzle her like that, I had the weirdest feeling of wanting to be him. What in the purple pork chop was comin' over me?

"Thank you for riding with me. I had a nice time," said Bella, on the way back to the house, "You're a good rider."

I could feel my face get real warm like it does when mama brags about me.

"Yeah, well I thought I was till I saw you. You ride like an Indian, like you're part of the horse."

She grinned at me and showed me these twinkles in her eyes that I was sure were special and no other boy had ever seen. Then I thought about it and decided that I'd bloody the nose of any boy that tried to.

"Well, silly, I am half Indian," she said with a little tee-hee laugh, and then she took my hand. "Let's see what mama's cookin'. She said we have to fatten you up, but you don't look skinny to me."

"I'm not skinny!" I snapped quickly. "I'm real strong. If I was fat like old Turtle from Bickford Street, I wouldn't be the fastest kid in school."

"Well, don't get mad, Eldridge. I didn't mean it as an insult. Who's Turtle from Bickford Street?"

"He's a smarty actin' fat kid that plays for the Bickford Snots. I …"

"The what?"

"The Bickford Snots. Their best player always has a runny nose, seems like, so that's why we started calling 'em the Snots. He can't hit my curve ball."

Sarah Bella laughed again. I loved hearing her laugh.

By the time we got back to the house, it was almost dark. Felton was in the kitchen with Margaret and Chief Wampooti. The kitchen smelled like pot roast, vegetables and other good stuff. It made me think of Aunt Bessie's kitchen on a Sunday after church. Margaret Two Cat was busy at the stove, and I was relieved that she wasn't cooking up some weird Indian food like roots or snails or something another awful like that.

"Well, I see you've already met Sarah Bella," Felton said when we came in, all cheerful and happy. Here we had driven a gazillion miles to bury Tyrane in a special grave, and we give up on it the minute we get here, and he acts like it ain't no big deal, damn him.

I gave him a dirty look and said coldly, "Yeah, so, where have you been?"

Felton grinned at me. "Makin' arrangements for the funeral. It's gonna be tomorrow. Between me and Chief Wampooti here, with a little help from our friends, it ought to be quite a show."

"You want a Dr. Pepper, Eldy?" Bella asked.

Even my name sounded special when she said it.

"Thanks," I said and accepted a tall, fizzing glass of soda.

"Chief says you're a little upset at me, Eldy. Is that true?" Felton asked.

I looked away and said nothing.

Chief Wampooti and Margaret watched me with a slight smile.

"Eldy, I ain't let you down yet, have I?"

His smile at me was different somehow. Mama used to smile that way when she would tease me about what I was gettin' for Christmas.

I looked at him, but quickly looked away again. What was he up to, teasin' me thataway about something as important as the funeral of our friend?

He repeated, "Well, have I?"

He hadn't, of course, but I wouldn't admit it.

Felton got up from the table where he had been sitting and stood looking down at me, his face very serious.

Sternly, he said, "Eldridge Brewer, Tyrane Percival was my best friend, as you know. I told you I wouldn't let him down again and I won't. That's all I'll say right now. You're just gonna have to trust me."

I listened to him, and I guess I decided to trust him, although I didn't see how there was any way we could bury Tyrane next to Leona LeSeur. The Funeral Director already told us he couldn't do it if Leona's brother wouldn't let us.

Then I remembered the calm way Felton anticipated the truck driver's actions at the rest stop, how he was in absolute control the whole time. The expression on his face now was the same as it was then, confident and in complete control.

That evening was just about the bestest time I ever had in my whole life, I reckon. First, there was the dinner Margaret cooked. It was a feast like nothin' I ever dreamt about and I ate till my belly was out to there, just like Chief said. He called the meat buffalo, but I knew it was beef. And, even if it was buffalo, I don't know how it could have been any better.

There was corn on the cob and some kind of stuff that was a Louisiana favorite. Everybody called it "jungle liar," or something like that. It was spicy hot and good as anything Mama ever cooked. The rice Margaret Two Cat fixed they called dirty rice, but dirty or not, it was super-duper.

Maybe everything tasted extra-specially good on account of Bella sitting next to me at one of the picnic tables.

She smelled like flowers and soap and … well, she smelled good.

Then there was the Chickasaw Village, which was what Chief called the back yard. The Chief had a way of making everything sound Indian.

When the festival got under way, the yard was lit up by hanging lanterns and lights strung in the trees. The Chief also built a huge bonfire in the middle of the yard.

"Braves dance around campfire like in old days, and brag about victories against Ho Non Wah Tribe enemies," he said.

Felton usually just grinned at such comments by Chief, but this time he rolled his eyes.

Finally, there were the people. They started showing up at about eight o'clock, and I soon figured out that most of 'em was musicians and some still performed. The Two Cat family greeted everybody warmly, led 'em to Banjo Man, and then introduced me as the new Fiddle Man.

"The great Fiddle Man, Tyrane Percival himself, anointed this young brave as successor," Margaret or the Chief would tell them as if it was earth-shattering news.

Among the guests were not one, but two Tweedlemans, the old man from the Not Forgotten Funeral Home that I had already met, and Ichthius Tweedleman IV, a younger version who was as white-skinned as the old man was and had only a few less wrinkles.

Sol Goldstein also showed up and brought poor Albert with him. The clerk looked like he'd recovered from his ordeal of finding himself face to face with a plastic-wrapped dead man in the company of what he probably thought was two serial killers.

Ruby Begonia also came. She had a radiant smile and gave it to me when Margaret brought her over.

She looked me up and down with an approving nod, and then said,

"Well, not bad, not bad at all. So you're the young man Tyrane taught to play the fiddle, huh?" She took my fingers in hers and looked at the hard calluses on my fingertips. "Do you like playing the fiddle, Eldridge Brewer?"

"Yes Ma'am, I love it. It—it makes me whole."

I had no idea where that thought came from, nor why I said it, nor even if it made any dadgum sense.

However, it meant something to Ruby Begonia. She nodded thoughtfully, cocked her head and smiled.

"He used to say that. I think Tyrane selected well. Yes, very well."

"Yes, Ma'am."

"They tell me you raised holy hell to make them send the Fiddle Man here to be buried next to Leona LeSeur."

I kicked a rock, feeling a little foolish and mumbled, "Yes, Ma'am."

"How'd you know about Leona?" she asked.

I told her about Tyrane's box, and added, "And, he used to play her song all the time. She had blue eyes."

Ruby said softly, "Yes, she did."

Someone called Margaret away, and she left Ruby Begonia with me.

She looked away for a minute, and when she looked back, there was a tear in her eye.

"I'd like to thank you, Eldridge Brewer. He meant a lot to me. I don't know what would have happened to me if it hadn't been for Tyrane Percival."

"I don't understand, Miss Begonia. You knew Tyrane when he was with the Funshiners, back then?"

She chuckled. "Oh, yes. Everybody knew your mentor, Eldridge Brewer. We were crushed when he disappeared. We knew he was broken up about Leona's death, but it never occurred to us that he would go to pieces. The first we knew, he was gone."

"Why?"

"Why? Well, we never knew. I ..."

"No, I mean, why did he mean so much to you? Were you his girl or something? Did you love him or something?"

She smiled sadly, and her eyes seemed to reverse and look inside.

"I loved him all right, but not like you think. I was just a little girl, eight years old, when I met him. You can say he probably saved my life. I was alone, homeless, living on the New Orleans waterfront when Tyrane found me and took me to Solomon Goldstein. He became like a father to me, and Tyrane was like my gentle uncle. He always came to the store to check on me when the band was in town. Sometime he brought me a trinket—not much, but something to let me know he thought about me. Yes, Eldridge Brewer, I loved your friend, Tyrane Percival."

"It's a flying wonder, ma'am, how I keep finding out about him doing something for somebody. Tyrane didn't talk about his self. He never said anything about you, or the Chief or even Felton Haliday. He was sad a lot, but when I asked what was wrong, he'd tell me to play a song on the fiddle." I surprised myself by not feeling stupid when I hesitantly added, "I loved him too."

"Yes, I can tell." She said and touched my cheek with two fingers.

Some of the people there had names that were familiar. A man in a colorful shirt introduced himself as Bobby Rydell. A black man named Lloyd Price in an electric blue suit grinned and waved at someone who called him "Stagger Lee." With the friendliest open smile, a chubby man asked me if Tyrane had taught me to do the twist. There were others, also, whose names tickled my memory.

About ten o'clock, Chief Wampooti stepped up on a platform raised about two feet off the ground, asked for everybody's attention and, with that great voice of his, immediately got it. There were about seventy people by then, and they all gathered round the huge Indian.

After swapping wise cracks with the crowd, Chief said, "This is special Powwow at Ho Non Wah Village. We gather tonight to honor departed brave for whom we have great feeling. He walked among us as Tyrane Percival, but we knew him as Fiddle Shaman, doer of wondrous deeds, and blood brother. On this night, we feel loss of friend, but we know he go to wondrous spirit world, a place of peace and harmony. We know loss, but we know joy, too. One of our own has returned to campfires."

I looked around at all the people, expecting some to snicker or roll their eyes at the way the Chief talked and at the glitzy way he waved his hands for emphasis, but no one did. They all stood looking sad and at attention as the big red man spoke.

"The Banjo Man has at last come back from the dark land. That land of sorrow and shame spat him out as too good and decent to reside with those in awful land of despair.

"My friends, Felton Haliday has returned bringing spirit of Fiddle Man, so we can properly send friend into spirit world to which all of us must someday go. This is cause for rejoicing!

"That would not be enough to overcome pain of losing great Shaman. However, Shaman himself knew that and, through power of spirit world, sent young Shaman he chose himself to walk as he did."

The Chief smiled at me and waved for me to come to him. There was a gentle nudge in my back, and when I turned, I found Felton pushing me with a kind of go-ahead, it's-all-right smile.

It seemed like there were a thousand people staring at me. My face burned, and I might have run for my life had it not been for one thing— well, two things actually. Those blue eyes of Sarah Bella Two Cat locked onto me, and suddenly I wasn't scared of nothing in the whole wide world. I boldly stepped forward and onto the platform.

Chief Wampooti draped an arm around me and said, "Oh great spirit of the Chickasaw, I present Eldridge Waymon Brewer, Shaman of the Fiddle."

Everybody began clapping enthusiastically, and I couldn't do anything but stand there and grin like a damn fool. Applause rained down on me for what seemed like forever, and then I felt something familiar pressed into my hands: the neck of Tyrane's fiddle and his bow.

On the raised platform, I looked down into the tear-filled eyes of Felton Haliday, who said huskily, "Play his fiddle, son. He can hear you tonight."

And, so I did.

Chapter Thirteen

The morning was overcast, and I thought I smelled rain, but Chief said it wasn't rain I smelled, but the odor of gases blowing off the bayous of Louisiana. He must have been right, because the clouds were quickly burned off by the rising sun, and I could see it would be a beautiful day.

Margaret put on the table a huge breakfast of eggs, bacon, and Cajun sausage, grits enough to feed the West Virginia National Guard, toast and coffee. She made me go for seconds but of course, it didn't take much persuasion.

Chief said, "Too much golden arch white man food. Too skinny. Need Chickasaw food. Make big and strong like Chief Wampooti."

Bella said, "Daddy, stop saying that. Eldy is not skinny. He's fine." She grinned at me.

"He sat on his horse like a fine Chickasaw brave yesterday. He's a good rider, too."

Felton laughed, "Well, Tyrane taught him to play the fiddle, but I seem to remember that he couldn't sit a horse worth a damn. Thank God he didn't teach him his way of riding, too!"

Everyone laughed. Margaret explained that one day all the Funshiners went riding between performances at a festival in Texas. All went well until Tyrane tried to get his horse to stop. The animal had other plans, and by the time they got him under control, Tyrane and his mount had wrecked the picnic grounds.

"Funshiners not get gig the next year," Chief added. "We keep Fiddle Man away from horses after that."

Felton stood up rubbing his belly. "Margaret, that was wonderful. C'mon, Eldy, there's some place we have to go this morning, and I don't want to be late."

"Can Bella and Whistler come?" I asked hopefully.

Felton shot a glance at Chief, who nodded, "You drive big wagon. Plenty room."

"Works for me," said Felton. "Eldy, take Whistler to the big wagon so he won't get excited when we go. If he does his musical recital after this big breakfast, we'll be in a mess."

We jabbered with each other about the evening's activities for a long time. It didn't occur to me to ask where we were goin', until I noticed airplanes coming in low.

"We must be near the New Iberia Airport," I said. "See those planes?"

"Yeah, Eldy, I see 'em." He smiled at me and shot a glance at Bella, who grinned, too.

I waited for more explanation, but none came. Instead, they both just grinned, and I swear it seemed like Whistler was grinning, too.

We have an airport in Jupiter Bluff, West Virginia, too. But at our airport, the landing strip ain't available May, June and July 'cause it's planted with beans and some corn too. During the growing season, the planes land on the dirt road that leads to the field. The terminal is a little blue cinder block building with two doors. The one on the left says "Office." On the other door, there's a picture of a toilet painted. The sign don't say MEN or WOMEN like most do. It says, ANYBODY, but at least it's a two-holer.

At the direction of a policeman, Felton pulled the Suburban to the curb where the place was crawling with people being picked up.

A plane must have just landed, because passengers hurried along with bags and suitcases, and uniformed porters pushed carts full of bags. Police directed cars that were in the way to move on, answered questions from travelers, and bustled about.

"What's goin' on, y'all? What in the flying flapjacks are we doin' out here?" I was getting pretty nervous. "This ain't funny, ya know."

"Relax, Eldy. You'll see in a minute," said Bella, her eyes merrily twinkling.

I gave her a dark look. It was the first time I had used the Eldridge evil eye on her, but it didn't seem to bother her.

"Keep your eyes peeled, Eldy," Felton said. "Somebody might need a ride from us. Look for somebody looking a bit lost. I told 'em what kind of car we'd be in, but in this hodgepodge …"

I scanned the crowd, feeling a little silly. Who was I looking for? I glanced at Whistler, who was intently watching the milling people. He gave me a quick look and lick, but both were very brief, as if he was afraid to take his eyes off the crowd lest he miss something. Then Whistler's tail began to wag, tentatively at first, and then more and more happily.

What in the world?

I flung the door open, jumped out of the car and ran across the platform, Whistler bounding alongside, probably farting like crazy, but I didn't care. When my Mama's arms wrapped around me, well, put it like this: I was glad to see her!

I felt little hands, too. Sometimes my little sister is a pain in the butt and makes me mad, but I loved her to death. Punky hugged herself to me, and I squeezed her back.

In the excitement of seeing Mama and Punky, I completely missed seeing Aunt Bessie, which is like not noticing a mountain. She joined in the reunion celebration too, nearly crushing me against her bosom.

Finally, Felton came over with Sarah Bella. I introduced the Chief's daughter, ignoring my little sister's smirk. She had figured me out pretty quick. We all gathered bags and climbed into the Suburban.

"Wait till you meet Chief Wampooti, Mama!" I said excitedly. "He's the absolutely coolest fella in the world, cool as the other side of a pillow. He's a real Chickasaw Indian and almost ten feet tall. He talks Indian, all the time too, don't he, Bella?"

Bella smiled and nodded. She was a mite bowled over with meeting my Mama, sister and aunt. I think I would have been too, so I understood why she was so quiet. I slipped my hand close and snaked my finger out to touch hers. My heart nearly burst when she slipped her hand into mine.

I learned later that Chief Wampooti Two Cat had paid for the flight, over Mama's objections. He said it was something he wanted to do for Tyrane and all of the Funshiners.

"It isn't charity, Mrs. Brewer. I'm repaying the thousands of kindnesses that Tyrane Percival did for people too numerous to count."

That time, it didn't sound like Indian talk to me.

I can't describe how glad I was to see my Mama after all me and Felton had gone through to get here, but something else thrilled me, too. It was the look on Felton's face when he saw Mama and the way her eyes softened when she looked at him. I wasn't imagining this, either. They could not stop looking at each other, smiling and touching. Maybe there was a chance Felton could become my Mama's boyfriend. Man, wouldn't that be something?

When we got back to the lodge, the Chief was nowhere to be seen. Margaret got Mama, Aunt Bessie and Punky settled in two rooms. I couldn't help but notice how Felton trailed after Mama, but then I realized that I was trailing after Sarah Bella too.

There wasn't a lot of time for talk. Me and Felton filled them in on our trip. Felton didn't tell her about me runnin' naked as a jaybird through Mega-Mart, and I didn't tell her about him and the boobies at the Best Plate Forward.

However, I couldn't resist telling Mama how much Felton liked maple syrup. His face reddened so much he had to duck out of the room.

Aunt Bessie was thrilled to learn that her brother was so well liked.

"He never would talk about his self much. I'd ask him about where he had been and all, but he wouldn't say nothing. Sometimes he looked so sad. I wanted to console him, but he wouldn't have it. He'd just go outside and play his fiddle. When you came over, Eldy, his face would light up."

I said softly, "They loved him here, Aunt Bessie. They really did."

We all got dressed for the funeral, Mama and Aunt Bessie in black dresses. Mama looked younger in her dress, while Aunt Bessie made me think of a big a black Volkswagen with white shoes. Punky put on a white dress and was a cute little pixie.

I was shocked when Felton came down. He was a different person, dignified and smart lookin', like a banker, or real estate agent, or maybe even a car salesman. He was dressed in a dark suit and tie, hair combed back nice and all, but what shocked me was that he had shaved off his beard and I swear he looked ten years younger, and downright handsome.

I put on a white shirt and stupid looking necktie Mama brought from home that I wear sometimes to church. It hung down below my belt but she made me wear it and I knew I could get shed of it later. She brought some pants too, but they were too short and I pitched a fit about wearing them and wore jeans instead.

In the kitchen, Felton called us all together, and without any words of explanation, said, "I got it set up to bury Tyrane next to Leona LeSeur. I hope it works, on account it was all me and Chief could come up with. Y'all don't get nervous. Just do what we tell you and it will all work out. Mary Elizabeth, you, Miss Bessie and Eldridge and little Ethel are gonna be in a limousine behind the hearse since y'all are family. Now, don't be alarmed if we do some crazy things, okay?"

"What about Whistler?" I asked.

"Don't worry about Whistler, Eldy. He'll be around. When we get to the funeral home, let Ichthius Tweedleman IV tell you what to do, and y'all do what he says. And, Eldy, I know you want to do something to Edwin LeSeur for what he's done, but don't you do nothing, you hear?

He's gonna get his."

I didn't say anything back. I hadn't figured out how yet, but I was gonna get that rotten asshole, and with more than a ham sandwich, too!

There weren't many people at the Not Forgotten Funeral Home, which kind of surprised me, since so many had come to the party the night before and swore they would be here today. Ruby Begonia, Sol Goldstein, and a few others I recognized from the night before were there but no one else. The Chief, Margaret, and Sarah Bella were nowhere to be seen. I didn't have time to worry about that though, 'cause of who else was there.

Quick enough, I recognized Edwin LeSeur sitting in his Lincoln limousine looking smug and smart-ass, and I recognized the man standing by his car. It was the biker the woman had pounded into the floor of Mega-Mart with a cast-iron frying pan. He was better dressed than at the Mega-Mart, I guess 'cause my pocketknife dismembered his leather pants. He wore a jacket too small, a tie too loose, and the too tacky snakeskin boots. Under his chauffeur's cap, I could see the edges of a bandage.

He glared daggers at me. If Mama hadn't been with me, I would have given him the finger. I settled for pulling back the corners of my mouth and sticking out my tongue at him.

Aunt Bessie looked distressed at the small turnout for the drive to the cemetery. She was already upset that we hadn't allowed for viewing and a chapel ceremony. Felton used all kinds of excuses, but none went very far with her, and she hardened toward Felton. He told me that we had to get to the burying as soon as possible, but he didn't tell me why.

Tweedleman said the casket was already loaded in the hearse and everyone should get in his or her car for the procession to the cemetery. "The preacher is going to meet our procession there," he said.

LeSeur stuck his head out of the window of his car and snapped disgustedly, "Procession? What damn procession? Just take the body out there. Let these people meet the damn hearse at the cemetery for Christ's sake. It'll take forever to drive the thirty miles out there."

Ichthius Tweedleman looked like a character in a horror movie caught peeing in the flowerpot in church.

"LeSeur," he snapped sharply, causing Edwin LeSeur to blush red as a beet, "you can spite your father and prohibit us from burying Tyrane Percival next to your sister, if you can live with it, but you will not trample on the dignity of a good man. I know you're only here to make sure nothing happens, but if you're going to participate in this ceremony, you'll shut your mouth!"

They herded us into the longest black limousine I had ever seen. It had seats facing front and back and even had a fancy bar in the middle.

Felton sat next to Mama across from Punky, Aunt Bessie, and me. I asked, "Where's Whistler? You said he could go to Tyrane's funeral. You promised."

I was trying to trust Felton, but so far, I hadn't seen anything to suggest that Tyrane wasn't headed for some cemetery in the boonies.

Felton smiled. "I did, and he will." He patted Mama's hand, lingering just a bit. Mama smiled at him.

The driver was the same fella who had greeted us the day before at the Not Forgotten Funeral Home, but he didn't seem befuddled now. Through the glass window separating the driver and front passenger from the rest of the car, he glanced back at Felton, who grinned at him as if he just ate somebody's chocolate. He started the engine, and I looked out the side window.

Ruby Begonia and several others had gotten into a black car, and there was a young blond woman I didn't recognize already in it. Sol Goldstein got in his late model Chrysler. I could see Albert behind the wheel with a grin on his face a mile wide.

The hearse pulled out with us right behind it, Ruby next, Sol's Chrysler and then LeSeur's Lincoln driven by LeSeur's man.

We paraded along about the same way they do at home when somebody dies. In Jupiter Bluff, the funeral processions get longer and longer, growin' all the way to the cemetery, 'cause each car they pass gets in behind the last car. Sometimes the processions get to be a mile long.

See, they do that in case the deceased is a relative they didn't know that they had, which in Jupiter Bluff is a whole lot more likely than you might think. They do that too in case the deceased is an ex-wife, which ain't as likely—or maybe it is.

We were getting to the end of downtown New Iberia when a ladder fire truck with bells, sirens and electronic whoops pulled out of a station about the time we was coming by.

A fireman standing in the street waved everyone through, except LeSeur and the cars behind his limo.

LeSeur's driver slammed on the brakes.

Then everything happened real fast. Our driver suddenly swerved the limo around a corner and floored it. I like to have jumped out of my skin as I grabbed Punky so she wouldn't fall off the seat. The battleship car hesitated and then shot forward like out of a gun barrel. I saw another limo like ours coming out of the side street that we were entering. Out the rear window, I saw both Ruby Begonia's and Sol Goldstein's cars behind us careening around the corner with us. Behind them, all I could see was the Fire Department ladder truck blocking the street and two cars like Ruby's and Sol's falling in behind the other limo.

Felton hollered, "Hang on, y'all, this is gonna be a wild ride! We ain't got a lot of time!"

Punky's eyes got big as pumpkins. After all, little girls don't get many chances to ride tail-on-fire all out in a car so long that you can hardly see the back seat. What's more, she didn't seem the least bit scared, although her little hand was gripping mine real hard.

I grinned at her. I should have known Felton had something good up his sleeve, and felt ashamed that I had doubted him.

Mama shouted, "What's happening, Felton?"

Face red with excitement, Felton replied, "We're goin' to a funeral, honey!"

Aunt Bessie wailed, "What're you doing, Mister Haliday? The hearse is back there!" When she twisted her big body to look out the window, she nearly smothered me in her bosom.

Felton laughed and replied to Aunt Bessie, "Yes, Ma'am, I know, and it's goin' all the way out to Greenshade Cemetery and Granite Quarry where a fella in a black frock coat is prepared to perform the last rites over an empty casket, if it goes that far before that pompous LeSeur figures out he's been had."

"Eldy, what's a granite quarry?" Punky asked.

My little sister knows I'm real smart and that I know things, so she always asks me stuff. I said confidently, "That's where they dig up those big tombstones, Punky. See, they dig up a stone, and it leaves a big hole in the ground. In Louisiana, they use the hole for a grave and they got the tombstone right there. They do sort of dumb things down here."

Punky looked at me as if I was a God or something. "Oh," She replied.

We were going pretty fast when we passed through a crowded open-air market on New Iberia's waterfront that seemed to go on forever. Music blared from loud speakers on both sides of the narrow street where vendors were selling stuff, making stuff, cooking stuff, and I don't know what the devil all else. The booths were decorated with balloons, ribbons and signs of all kinds and description. The air smelled like cooked and raw crab, shrimp and crawfish.

Felton pushed a button on the console activating the window, which went down with a smooth swish. "You know where we're goin, don't ya? 'Cause I ain't got no idea!" He hollered at the driver.

"Yes sir!" the driver yelled over his shoulder as he swerved to avoid a fish cart someone was pushing across the street.

The limo just clipped the front of it as we went by, and I saw fish and ice go slicking across the pavement and the man pushing it shake his fist at us.

The driver said, "Mister Tweedleman said I was to take y'all to the bandstand on the south end of the Park and to be damn quick about it, which is why I'm hauling ass!"

"How long will it take LeSeur to get to the granite quarry, Felton?" I asked.

"Maybe an hour, then thirty minutes to get back."

As we drove into the park, I heard what sounded like a brass band playing to the mournful rhythm of a big drum. I listened a minute trying to recognize the tune and in a few seconds, I knew it was "Nearer My God to Thee." It was played slow and mournful, like at a funeral. Felton patted my hand and said, "He's gettin' one hell of a send-off, Eldy."

In front of the limo loomed the rear of a bandstand with white banisters around the stage. The music was much louder and coming from the other side.

The driver stopped the limo, and we all piled out. Ruby Begonia and her passengers got out of their car grinning at Felton. Sol Goldstein parked behind them. Goldstein carried an odd-shaped package under his arm.

Felton didn't give anybody time for no greetings nor nothing else either, but hurried around the red brick bandstand, the rest of us trailing behind.

We came around the building and stopped dead together like we were connected. Four pairs of eyes stared at a spectacle we wouldn't have imagined in our wildest dreams. Now I know it's hard to believe, knowing how I always got something to say, but I was speechless other than, "Holy shit!"

Mama didn't fuss at me for the "s" word, probably 'cause she thought that too!

If Peepee believes any of the things I tell him about this trip, it sure ain't gonna be this part. There was a crowd of maybe fifty to seventy-five people, a lot of 'em in wild masks and brightly colored costumes, even clowns and demons. They swayed or danced a kind of sorrowful jig or walked in place, sort of a parade with no place to go. Startling as the crowd was, it was nothing compared to everything else.

Chief Wampooti Two Cat of the Big River Chickasaw was sitting king-like on the Hanoverian horse I had seen in the stable. He was magnificent in full dress Indian stuff. Feathers of red, green and yellow flowed down his back from a huge beaded headdress. He wore cloud-white buckskin decorated with shiny brass and silver. His massive face was painted pure white with two red paint slashes above each eye. He looked fierce! Braced against the pommel of his saddle was a long lance with three enormous feathers at the base of the shining steel tip. A blue and white striped blanket under a silver-spangled saddle covered the horse's flanks.

Margaret Two Cat, also in white buckskin with sparkling silver things, sat on a smaller version of the Chief's enormous horse. She wore ostrich feathers with soft, flowing plumes and her hair was plaited in a ponytail tipped with two yellow feathers. She sat astraddle—no sidesaddle for the wife of a great chief. The blanket on her horse was exactly like her husband's, and she sat her horse with the same royal bearing. There was a blue and red finger-painted mark on each cheek and her dark skin gleamed in the sun.

Then there was Sarah Bella, who would have been a beautiful princess in King Arthur's court, if he had been an Indian. My heart just about pounded out of my chest seeing her on the pinto pony she had ridden with me the evening before. She, too, wore white buckskin with silver spangles flashing in sunlight raying through the trees. Pigtails hung on each side of her face, as if it was so perfect only spun black diamonds could frame it right. The white buckskin skirt rode up enough for me to see slender muscular legs grip the sides of the little pony with ease.

I wondered again if all of this was a fairy tale dream, conjured up in my imagination. Watching Sarah Bella Two Cat, I thought I must be coming to the end of my dream where I'm the prince and live happily ever after with my true love. You know, like Snow White or Cinderella.

But, it wasn't a dream.

Chief Wampooti was real, Margaret and Sarah Bella were real, and Mama, standing beside me saying, "She's the loveliest thing I've ever seen," was real. That awful pain in my gut that was with me for so long after my Daddy died was gone now, and that, too, was real.

As soon as we showed up, some of Wampooti's "Indian braves" hustled us over to a throng of people who were singing and chanting. They followed a fat man riding backwards in a brightly-colored wagon pulled by two stubby horses. He wore a shimmering white suit and a white hat with a long feather in the brim. He beat slow and steady on a massive drum with a round bottom like a kettle. Costumed musicians played instruments from flutes to tambourines, adlibbing hymns like "Free As A Bird," and "A Closer Walk with Thee." They played the hymns in cross rhythm to the march, but somehow it all came out with a kind of uplifting joy.

Chapter Fourteen

Felton hurried me to the front of the procession.

"C'mon, Eldy, we got to hurry up!" he shouted above the din. "They can't start without us."

I was overwhelmed. He had to grab my hand and pull me along as if I was Punky.

I hollered as I looked around, "What about Mama and Punky and Aunt Bessie, Felton?" The crowd had swallowed them up. "I got to look after them. They don't know nothin' about all this here stuff. They could get lost."

"They won't get lost, Eldy. I promise. Ruby Begonia is looking after them."

About then I saw the Chief's hippie wagon with its slogans and tailpipe belching clouds of black smoke. It pulled up alongside Ruby and the rest of my family.

Watching them clamber into the hippie bus, another question suddenly struck me, and I asked Felton, "Where's Tyrane?"

Felton grinned and pointed. "There."

The pea-green Studebaker pickup, driven by one of the men I met the night before, was leading the procession, and it was to the truck Felton was hurrying me.

Felton hollered, "We're supposed to ride in the lead!"

Covered with so many flowers you could barely see it, Tyrane's casket leaned against the truck's cab. The kiddy pool had been placed on the upper end of the casket to look like a jaunty French cap. Azaleas, roses and other flowers were on top of the plain pine casket. In the middle was a blown up picture of Tyrane in a white suit with his fiddle.

Old Whistler was having the time of his life in the truck, running around the casket barking and farting at the horses and weird people. I was glad there was a good breeze, 'cause excited as he was, the air downwind would not have supported human life.

Felton and I got into the back of the truck, and Whistler gave my face a good washing and greeted Felton with equal joy. I was laughing with delight. He whistled, but Felton grinned and said, as he fondled the dog's big shaggy head, "I never thought I'd be glad for that, but I am today." A worried look flashed across his face, but he quickly covered it.

I wondered how long before LeSeur figured out that he had been snookered and was crawling along behind an empty hearse, and how long would it take him to race back this way? How long would it take us to get to Shady Acres Cemetery where the LeSeur gravesites were located?

The noisy procession wound slowly through the park. People stopped whatever they were doing and watched the show, as we snaked by like a giant Chinese dragon. There was several pick-up softball games going on, and near a pretty duck pond, couples were picnicking on blankets spread out on the grass. Men were flinging Frisbees back and forth to each other or to dogs that jumped high in the air to catch them.

I tried to teach Whistler to do that, and it worked in a manner of speaking. The trouble was I couldn't throw it but once, because when Whistler caught the Frisbee, he saw it as his property to destroy. There was no catching him. He usually took it under the house where he proceeded to shred it like the dozen or more Frisbees already there.

People stood with hands on their hearts as we mournfully, yet somehow happily, went by. I couldn't imagine them not being shocked at the sight of us, but they didn't seem at all surprised—curious maybe, but not surprised.

Everything was so perfect. Mama was there and making eyes at Felton, Sarah Bella had held my hand, Aunt Bessie had reason to be proud of her late brother, and he would finally rest beside the woman he loved. I was participating in a funeral parade honoring a man who it turned out was something of a saint.

So why did I feel troubled?

Besides the Chief, his wife, and Sarah Bella, there were other riders, all in costume. Bella's pinto danced along, often sideways, and as she drew close, I waved at her and got a big grin in return. She cantered over to the truck, stretched out her hand for me, and when I grabbed it, she hauled me into the saddle behind her. I whooped as we pealed aside to gallop along outside of Chief Wampooti.

Bella and I broke away after a few minutes at my insistence.

"Where is the graveyard?" I shouted into her ear. "How much further is it to the grave?"

She had to wait a minute before answering because about that time the Chief hollered a war whoop that would drown out the roar of a jet plane.

She pointed across the park toward where a small but fancy wrought iron gate opened into the back of the cemetery.

"Through those gates and then a hundred yards or so," she shouted. "The LeSeur graves are on the south side of the cemetery."

She reined the horse away from the noise so we could hear ourselves think. "What's the matter?" She asked, looking worried.

"I don't really know. The last time I had a feeling like this, me and old Peepee got caught sneakin' into the peep show at the carnival. I got a whuppin', but good. I just have a bad feeling is all."

Bella told me earlier that Shady Acres Cemetery dated back to the 1700s and was a popular tourist site because of its fancy tombs and graves, more than half of them, above ground. Over the years, she said, a craft fair and flea market had grown up outside the cemetery's rear entrance until it now stretched several blocks along the street in both directions.

The sun flashed on chrome handlebars, twirling spokes, and a shiny helmet. It was a boy 'bout old as me coming from the cemetery's back gate and pedaling his bicycle like his ass was on fire.

The boy stared up at us, eyes bulging. I think he was shocked and actually a little scared.

"It's all right," I assured him. "Did you just come from the gate over yonder?"

After a moment's hesitation, in which I figured he was scared that maybe he done something wrong, he nodded. He acted like his pants was full of ants.

"Lemme ask you something, and then I'll let ya go. While you were at the flea market, did you see any ratty lookin' bikers that never seen soap suds in their whole dirty life and wearing ugly snake skin boots?"

"No, I didn't go to the flea market like I usually do. That's where I was headed until I seen the procession over at the bandstand. I figured I could catch up to it by circling through the back gate. That's when I saw you and the, uh, Indian girl."

"Princess. She's a Indian Princess." I corrected.

His eyes got big as moon pies as he put a ragged sneaker on a pedal and exclaimed, "Aw, man, she is, really?"

"Yes, and you better get goin' now 'cause me and her have Princess stuff we got to do."

When he hesitated, I tossed one of her shiny spangles to him and urged, "Go on now!"

He caught it and cried, "Wow!"

I was thinking of those ugly asshole bikers from the Mega-Mart. LeSeur's driver wouldn't be in New Iberia alone. I bet Leona's brother hired them all and the rest of that rat pack was probably somewhere around.

"What's the matter?" Bella asked as we galloped off toward the gate leaving the boy standing in awe. I bet he told everybody he knew about meeting a real live Indian Princess. I bet he used the spangle in "Show and Tell".

"We got to check out the flea market. Remember me telling you about the bikers in Crossover Alabama?"

"Why would they be here?"

"LeSeur's driver was one of 'em. He must have hired them in case we tried something. I figure there's a good chance the others might be hanging around this flea market."

I pointed at a wall of orange azaleas at the gate. "Let's ride in there behind the bushes and tie him off!"

Trying to look casual, we strolled in front of the booths, looking for those telltale boots.

"Sometimes they have pony rides, and fire engine rides for the kids," Bella explained. "I think they alternate a miniature train ride around the parking area with balloon rides. This must be balloon Saturday."

There was a hot air balloon as big as a two-story house tied to three stakes and wafting in the breeze. I started to get one of my ideas.

I kept my head down as we moved among the people poking around in the booths.

It didn't take long. Arguing with a vendor over the price of an awful painting—Elvis Presley in a white suit on black felt—was Crooked Teeth, even though the guy at Mega-Mart hadn't left enough teeth to be crooked. The other two, Stinky and Crew Cut were right beside him.

We ducked into a booth next to them.

"That's them," I whispered. "We got to find out where they parked their bikes."

"On the other end of the street is where they make 'em park motorcycles."

I had no idea what I was going to do. But, I was going to do something. I might as well admit I am bit by the angel of devilment because it's in my nature to snooker assholes!

The motorcycles were parked inconveniently along the back line of the lot, not far from the hot air balloon. I hurried to them and picked out the three with snake decals on the gas tanks and fenders.

"You keep watch. I'm gonna see if there's some way to strand 'em," I told Bella.

"What?"

"You know, steal their horses. It won't stop 'em, but it'll slow their asses down. Not only that, I owe the sons of bitches for makin me moon everybody in Crossover, Alabama while running through a damn Mega-Mart."

I went to the nearest of the bikes, a late model Harley dirt bike. Its gas tank was locked, as I was afraid it would be which meant sugar or sand in the gas tank was out. Releasing air in the tires wouldn't help either, because modern bikes carried air pumps.

While standing by the bikes scratching my head, I studied the hot air balloon. A yellow rope ran from stakes around the basket, and a sign in the roped off waiting area nearby read Next Rise – 2:00 P.M.

I knew the way these balloons worked, on account of Jupiter Bluff Junior High Principal, Hecktor Munsenmeyer. Hot air balloons were his big thing, a hobby, ya know. He brought his balloon to the school Monday before every Thanksgiving holiday and gave all the kids with the best grades a ride. "Monkey Myer" (that's what we called him) made a big deal of explaining all the scientific stuff involved like hot air rising and all that.

Oh, Lordy, Eldy.

I gazed back and forth at that great balloon and over at those snakeskin bikes, and could almost hear old Peepee doing his broken English imitation when he wants to be funny, "Eldy Brewer, you crazy American. You not do dumb thing. You crazy!"

This time, I thought, Peepee was right. I am crazy!

"How long is your saddle rope, Bella?"

"Forty-five feet, I guess. What are you gonna do?" She looked at me, worried.

"Well, not that it's gonna do a lot of good but at least their sorry butts will be on foot unless they can fly. I'm gonna airmail their motorcycles to Texas by hot air balloon!"

A few minutes later, I was in the basket with my hand on the valve to open up the gas-fired air heater, which I knew would make a God-awful roar and bring people running when they saw the balloon rise. Here goes nothing, I thought, and I spun the valve wide open.

For just a second, nothing happened, but then there was a woomph sound, and the heater roared. A great flame spewed into the opening of the balloon.

Bella stood by one of the two remaining tie-downs with my pocketknife.

"Cut 'em! Cut 'em!" I shouted over the roar.

She gave me a you-sure-about-this? kind of look then cut the two ropes with a single slash to each.

"Oh shit!" I yelled.

I was almost twenty feet in the air before I could blink.

I clambered over the side of the basket and began shinnying down the rope where I had tied the three motorcycles like on the tail of a kite.

Bella jumped up and down and shouted at me to hurry. What did she think I was gonna do, straddle one of the motorcycles and soar off into the distance like ET on his little basket bicycle? I thought old Peepee would be doubled over with laughter watching me trying to get out of that basket. Out of the corner of my eye, I could see a few people move toward the Balloon rides. Maybe they thought the rides were starting early.

Every second it felt like the balloon rose a hundred feet. The ground was drawing away like a rock falling in a well. I frantically climbed past the first and second bike to sit on the third. I was still thirty feet in the air and desperately looked for some place to jump, some place soft maybe.

Suddenly, I saw the only chance I had. It was a stake-bodied truck parked at the end of the parking area, about half-full of string-tied bales of pine straw.

There wasn't time to think should I or shouldn't I? I Hollered "HOOOOLEEEEY SHIIIIIIT!" and jumped off the motorcycle, aiming at the straw.

Well, I landed in the straw all right, but it was a lot harder than I expected. I tried to collapse and fall as I landed, the way Burt Reynolds did one day on a TV show, but when I hit the straw, a terrible sharp pain shot up my left leg.

"Damn!" I cried.

Bella ran to the truck, her face white.

"Eldy, oh Eldy!" she cried.

She grabbed my arm as I started to fall when I put weight on my left ankle. I didn't know whether it was broken or not, but it hurt like a thousand needles.

I looked across the parking lot. People were running and pointing at the balloon sixty or seventy feet in the air, the three bikes dangling from the basket. Each looked like a shiny bow tie as the sun glistened off the polished chrome.

"Help me down," I pleaded to Bella. "We got to get outta here!"

When I hit the pavement, I cried out but gritted my teeth through it and hobbled into the azaleas leaning on Sarah Bella. We got on the horse and took off across the park. Each gallop sent shooting pains through my ankle.

Behind me, I heard a high-pitched voice scream, "That's my bike! That's my bike!"

We waved the Studebaker to a stop. I slid off the horse too confidently and nearly fell on my face when I put weight on my ankle. Tears of pain ran down my cheeks.

"It's his ankle, Papa!" Sarah Bella shouted to her father who had come to see why we were riding so hard and fast. His first concern was for Bella, of course, but he quickly saw I was the cause for concern.

Felton helped me into the truck bed and checked my ankle.

"Eldy, what happened? One minute you and Bella were here and then you were gone."

I squeezed my eyes closed against the pain, unable to speak until it subsided a little, but I did manage to give a weak grin and point toward the west.

"I got 'em back, Felton, those biker assholes from the Mega-Mart. They're gonna have to learn to fly!"

Everyone looked where I pointed and saw the balloon soaring hundreds of feet in the air, motorcycles flashing like sun on a jet plane. In spite of the pain in my ankle, I was real pleased with myself. I thought, dadgum it, it's a shame old Peepee couldn't be here to see it. He would have appreciated the sight of those dangling motorcycles.

With my Mama worriedly watching, Felton said that my ankle was not broken but badly sprained. He wrapped it while he and Chief discussed what they should do about this new development. In the end, they decided there wasn't anything to do but hurry the procession to the graveyard.

Forty minutes later, we were there. Ichthius Tweedleman at the Not Forgotten Funeral Home was out of canopies, so we had had to get our own. The Chief told Felton that that was "no problem." I think if Felton had known what the Chief was gonna use for one, he would have called it a big problem. It was too late now, and I guess it didn't really matter, anyway.

What the Chief came up with was something that he used for

tailgating on Sundays when the Saints were in town. It was a huge canvas thing, held together by aluminum pipes which shaped it into a New Orleans Saints football helmet. It was positioned so that the grave was where the face guard would have been.

Some of Chief Wampooti's "braves" were the pallbearers. After they put the casket on the straps above the grave, they stepped back and stood stiffly in line with their arms crossed the way Indians do at a big tribal ceremony, which of course this kind of was. Everybody else gathered around as a preacher named Henri Briox stood beside Tyrane's pine casket. As Tyrane's only family, Aunt Bessie in her black mourning dress, Mama, Punky and me sat in a line of chairs in the front. Felton was given a place of honor, too and no one objected.

Whistler quickly found out that the cemetery had a thousand squirrels, hundreds of rabbit holes, and more concrete things to pee on than he had pee to pee on 'em. He went romping off over and between grave markers and tombstones, panting and barking at first one rabbit hole and then another.

Reverend Briox began his funeral sermon and I did my funky fast ball best to pay attention, but he sounded as if he had done it so many times, he could've done it in his sleep.

He began in a high, squeaky voice, "Dearly beloved, we are gathered here in the Shady Rest Cemetery to lay to rest a departed soul ..."

The poor preacher ain't even got to askin' for his first amen when the little metal folding chair Aunt Bessie was sitting on decided it had had enough, and with a gentle flutter sank slowly into the soft earth rolling poor Aunt Bessie over like a great blob of black Jello. Everybody rushed to help her, which is a good thing on account of it took four men to get her upright again. In a few minutes, they replaced her chair with a bench they got from the walking path that wound through Shady Rest Cemetery.

I looked over all the faces and found Ruby Begonia, who smiled at me almost as fondly as Mama did. Standing beside her was a pretty blonde woman of about thirty in a business suit, and next to her was a skinny little old lady in a black dress who seemed like she was a bit lost. On Ruby's right was Sol Goldstein with that peculiar package under his arm. Albert was there too, wide-eyed at what was going on around him.

Several faces were familiar from the evening before. A man who played guitar for a few years with the Funshiners stood next to another former band member Felton had introduced to me as "Dumbo," like the flying elephant. He had ears big enough to fly, or at least get him off the ground, if he could wiggle 'em fast enough. He was the piano man at the time the Funshiners disbanded.

After all the confusion of Aunt Bessie's collapsing chair, the preacher got his bible out again, adjusted his face for a funeral and began again.

"Dearly beloved, we are gathered here today to lay to rest a departed soul, a friend, a brother and ..."

The minute I heard the sirens, I knew we done fell through the septic tank sure enough! Them sirens were coming this way and it sounded like every police car in Louisiana was involved in a high-speed chase. They drowned out Preacher Briox's reedy voice. Felton and me turned around at the same time, and I'm sure I looked just as upset as he did. The disappointment in his expression was awful.

Scattering the pea gravel of the narrow lane was LeSeur's limo last seen waiting for a fire department ladder truck. There were motorcycles on each side and a County Sheriff's cruiser behind. Barely visible, the snakeskin gang members were coming out of the Azaleas at the gate.

LeSeur's limo came to a noisy stop behind the mourners, showering some of them with pea gravel off the walkway. Preacher Briox's sermon died a second time before he asked for his first "amen."

He looked at all the furor with a face that looked ready to cry and his lips mouthed, "My God, What now?"

Chapter Fifteen

Edwin LeSeur was red-faced and mad enough to eat his own drawers
when he jumped out of the limo even as the car rocked from the sudden
stop. He swept his hand around to cover everybody in the whole flyin'
world and screamed like a Cajun maniac.

"Arrest these people! Arrest these people!"

He ran across graves twixt us and his fancy car, actin' like he'd lost his
feeble mind! He waved his arms back and forth like a referee blowing
his whistle over a fumble at a football game. He stumbled over the curb
marking the edge of his family graveyard and I was some disappointed
that he didn't go ass over teakettle. It would've tickled the pickle out of
me if he'd got his self a face full of cockleburs.

The motorcycle cops got off their black and white bikes with hot-stuff
attitudes. You could tell they thought they were hot pookey popsicles the
way they hitched up nightsticks and gun belts and walked around like
general Patton.

Out of the cruiser stepped a heavyset uniformed officer, who moved
like somebody in charge. I knew right off that this cowboy wasn't no
Cogdil Brubaker worried about Alabama hunters shootin' Tennessee
deer out of season. I didn't think we could run a wing-dingy on this one.

When he got to the graveside under the football helmet, LeSeur's
face was so red that I thought for a minute it might bust into flame.

"You people are desecrating the graves of my family!" he snarled. "I'll
see you put under the jail for this, you—you ghouls!"

He turned to the biker that drove the limo, "Take this damn box off
my family's graveyard, right now! Get it outta here! Sons of bitches!
Jesus Christ, a football helmet!"

Felton Haliday was on his feet, as was everybody else. He charged toward LeSeur, fists clenched.

"Wait a minute, LeSeur. This is the funeral of a good man who lived a good life. He loved your sister and she loved him. Your father wanted him buried here."

I watched for him to chomp off a big plug of tobacco to load up his weapon, but he didn't. Damn!

LeSeur turned to the Sheriff's uniformed deputy and commanded, "Do your duty, Sheriff! Arrest these people. Be careful of the Indian, he's violent."

Then he turned and looked at me. I glared back with the meanest, nastiest, evilest eye I could make. It would've fried a cow chip. His head popped back like I caught him a good upper cut, and he added viciously, "And put that conniving little bastard in a damn cage."

One of the motorcycle policemen moved toward me, but stopped dead in his tracks when the Chief's lance stuck him in his butt. One of Chief's braves trotted forward and seemed ready to nock an arrow in his bow.

Turning back to Felton, LeSeur said, "You're not gonna bury this bastard in my family's graveyard. Lieutenant, I demand that you arrest these people for desecration of my family's graveyard."

I about lost it then. Ignoring the shooting pain in my ankle, I started at him. I kicked Fatso's butt on Bickford Street last fall and I thought, by God I'll kick this asshole's too! I didn't know how I was going to do it, truth be told, only that I had to try. I ain't gonna let nobody talk like that about Tyrane.

Mama and Aunt Bessie grabbed and held me. I was eat up with a rage that was making me crazy.

"Let me go! Dammit, Mama, let me go!" I shrieked, "He called Tyrane a bastard. By God, I'm gonna beat the shit out of this son of a bitch!"

It was a long time later that I realized how I cursed and that mama didn't slap it out of me!

Since I couldn't hit LeSeur, I threw the winners of me and Peepee's insult contests at the bastard.

"You're—you're dumber than a box of hair. If my dog was as ugly as you, I'd shave his ass and make him walk backward!" I remembered still another. "Your mama eats road kill 'cause she's the onliest one knows how to fix it."

"All right, that's enough. Sit down kid." The all-business officer from the cruiser snapped at me.

But, you know, I heard some snickers from the crowd, and a grin passed across his face too.

To Felton and LeSeur who were glaring at one another, he said, "You! Sit down! You too, LeSeur. I'm sorry, Reverend Briox, but we've got to stop this ceremony. This is the LeSeur family grave, and this man claims he did not approve the burial of—he glanced at a note pad—Tyrane Percival here." He glanced nervously at Chief Wampooti, but I think he figured the giant wouldn't impale anybody, at least for a while.

Aunt Bessie got up off her bench, blobbed forward like a sumo wrestler and grabbed LeSeur's sleeve.

Madder 'n hell, she said, "Just who do you think you are charging in here like this? This is the funeral of my beloved brother, and I'll thank you to leave us alone!"

LeSeur rounded on poor Aunt Bessie and snarled to one of the snakeskin gang, "Who the hell is this? Somebody get this fat walrus off of me!"

The biker gang moved forward as if they were gonna grab hold of my Aunt. I don't think they realized that it would take all of 'em just to get their arms around her!

"Chief!" called Felton sharply.

Holding his lance up with feathers fluttering in the breeze, Chief Wampooti trotted toward the bikers. Now lemme tell ya, that was a scary lookin' thing and I swear I could hear their assholes goin' thoup, thoup, thoup!

At nearly 'bout seven feet tall his self and on the hugestest horse anybody had ever seen, he was a fearsome towering sight. Them bikers started shivering like they was in a ice box naked. They fell back from him and parted a little bit, but the big horse herded them back together as if they was cows.

I'm sure they had to go somewhere later and change their underwear.

Chief leaned across the pommel, patted the tomahawk in his sash and told them in that big voice, "I am Chief Wampooti Two Cat of the Ho Non Wah Tribe of the Big River Chickasaw. I not take filthy scalps of rotten unwashed bikers. If gang stay, I cut off heads to put on posts for tribal ceremony!"

I would have laughed if things wasn't so wrung-up tense.

The bikers stared white-faced for a moment, glanced at the limo driver like to tell him, "You can stay if you want to, but we're getting' the hell outta here!"

The next thing I knew they were running across the park, lookin' back like the Indians were gonna come after 'em with bows strung with arrows.

The police lieutenant said to Felton, "I'm sorry, sir. I'll have to take you and these others into custody until we can straighten this mess out. I don't like breaking up a funeral like this, but it is abundantly clear that you can't go on with this ceremony. You don't have permission to inter your friend here."

Felton must have seen that this policeman was not dumb as a post like old Brubaker, because he was not trying to snooker him.

"Lieutenant," Felton said calmly, "we do have permission to bury Mister Percival in this exact location of this graveyard. It was granted to us by LeSeur's father before he passed away."

The Lieutenant thought about that for a moment, a moment in which I had a sense that he might be a little bit on our side. He looked at LeSeur as if expecting him to argue about it.

Instead, LeSeur snapped, "Get it done, Officer. Proof of their criminal behavior is all around you. A football helmet, for God's sake. Fruitcakes running around in Indian costumes. I'll not have this on the sacred remains of my family. Arrest these evil creatures!"

Reluctantly, the Officer reached for handcuffs on his belt. Aunt Bessie wailed like a goblin, "Oh no. Oh no, my poor brother. What's going to happen to my poor brother?"

Felton pleaded. "Wait a minute, Lieutenant. Lieutenant …" He looked closer at the name badge on the policeman's chest. "Lieutenant Custer. I don't think you…"

He stopped and stared again at the nameplate.

"Oh shit," he muttered. He looked fearfully at the milling Indians and at Chief Wampooti and said, "This can't be happening. Your name is G. Custer, as in General George Custer?"

At about then, Chief Wampooti rode up to loom over the scene like out of a comic book. He froze for an instant when he heard Felton say "General Custer." He and the horse were so still, they looked like a statue, and then a great smile spread across that fierce white painted face. He whooped louder than ever and raised the lance over his head, turned to his "braves" and shouted excitedly, "We take many scalps on this great day!"

Chapter Sixteen

I don't know what might have happened next if things hadn't got interrupted when they did. Lieutenant Custer frantically clawed at his gun. However, like old dumb Cogdil Brubaker, he forgot about the safety loop. The other two cops didn't know whether to run, jump or sing Dixie. They were surrounded by Indians on horseback sidling their horses tight upon them. One of the Indians was my princess.

Edwin LeSeur was scared out of his socks. His face was white as mama's best tablecloth. It turned even whiter when the point of Chief's lance touched his belly just above the belt buckle.

Aunt Bessie wailed, "Oh, my poor brother, Tyrane!"

Mama grabbed Punky and held her close, the way the woman always does in the street of a cowboy movie when the gunslingers are flexing their fingers over their guns.

Me? All's I can say is I was doin' my de-double damndest not to pee my pants!

"Here now!" a voice shouted, "Order! Order!"

It was not a particularly loud voice, but it sure had a ring like you better squat if it said "pookey!"

Everybody stopped what they was doing like God's voice had boomed out of the sky. Boy, that place got quiet as a cemetery. I know, it was a cemetery, but it got quieter yet. There was only one sound; a long perfect e-flat whistle from Whistler, near exhausted from chasin' squirrels and rabbits and come to see what all the commotion was about.

We all turned to see a dignified lookin' black gentleman, about fifty, walking toward us from a limousine as big as LeSeur's.

He had broad shoulders, was about tall as Felton, and wore a gray suit that must have cost as much as his car. His hair was salt and pepper, kind of favoring the salt, and cut real close until it looked like a thin layer of steel wool. His face was stern, eyes piercing like to go through you. His thick lips were set as he stalked up the rise to the front, where everyone fell away from him not a little awed, especially the policemen.

I could hear off in the distance some kids playing ball across the nearby park. I even heard a blue jay screech at another bird.

Arriving at the casket, he stuck his hand out to Felton first.

"I'm sorry I'm so late," he said to Felton. "I tried to get here sooner, but traffic and all that, you know."

Felton stared at the newcomer, then seemed to relax. He was about to speak when something in the man's eyes stopped him.

"I'm Circuit Court Judge Skyler Boudreaux," the new fella went on hurriedly.

It come to me like a flash: Tyrane throwing the Grand ole Opry agent in a mud puddle for refusing to let his bass player perform because he was black. Wasn't "Skyler" the Funshiner bass player's first name? For some reason it seemed he didn't want LeSeur to know he knew Felton.

The Judge went on. "I'm told there is a dispute over where to bury the man they call Fiddle Man, Tyrane Percival. I knew Mister Percival— quite well, too, I might add. I thought I might be of some service. It would certainly be a travesty to put to rest any man with such a cloud over his burial, and particularly a man of such decency as Tyrane Percival."

He still didn't wait for an acknowledgement from Felton, and the glance he shot at Chief Wampooti made him hold his water too.

Turning to LeSeur, he said, "Counselor, is it my understanding that you are prohibiting the burial of Percival here?"

I thought, "Counselor?" Ain't that what they call lawyers? I knew LeSeur was a snake, but I didn't think he was that lowdown of a snake!

LeSeur found his tongue after the long stare he gave Boudreaux when he got there. Just as mad as before, he said, "You're damn right I am, Judge Boudreaux. And I'm bringing criminal charges against these bastards for desecrating my family's graves. Look what they've done!"

Boudreaux nodded and looked around.

"I see." he said, turning to Felton. "Now tell me, why do you think that you have permission to bury Mister Percival here in spite of Mister LeSeur's refusal to allow it? Do I have that right?"

I was getting to know Felton so well that I could sometimes tell what he was thinking. Right then, I knew he was thinking: What the hell is going on here? Was this man on his side or not?

Felton replied, "Yes sir, I do. His father, the late Edwin Sr., you might say gave us permission."

Boudreaux nodded, looked at the Indians next, and to Chief Wampooti said, "You sir, on the horse. Who are you?"

The huge Indian drew himself up, stood the lance straight up, pounded his massive chest and with utmost dignity bellowed, "I am Chief Wampootiteepa, Ho Non Wah Tribe, Big River Chickasaw, blood brother to Eagle, Drum Shaman. I send great warrior, Fiddle Man to new happy music place, I—"

"All right, all right, Chief, I know," the Judge interrupted, waving impatiently. "That's enough. I got it."

I couldn't swear to it, but I think a grin flashed across the Judge's face, but if anyone else saw it, I don't know.

"Chief Wampooti," Judge Boudreaux went on, "I would appreciate it if you and your braves would dismount. Your milling horses are only adding to the confusion."

To the policemen, he said, "Gentlemen, I do not intend to disrupt this funeral anymore than it has been already. Please holster your firearms and be easy. In other words, chill out, okay?"

The judge pinched his chin like he was studying the situation, making up his mind. "Let me see now, we need some officers of the court here, so I'll make some appointments before we get started."

He pointed at the towering mounted Indian.

"Chief Wampooti, you'll serve as our Bailiff. Rev. Briox, I'm appointing you as temporary Clerk of Court since you have a bible and presumably, a direct line to the Almighty. We'll need both when you swear in witnesses. I—"

"What? Wait a minute." LeSeur interrupted. "Witnesses ... what witnesses?"

LeSeur had been confident that the police would arrest us. When the Judge showed up, his confidence started pealing away like sunburned skin on his nose.

"Surely, Counselor, you know what witnesses are. I know you don't get in a courtroom very often, but—"

"Well, I know what a damn witness is, you big—"

He stopped himself and his face turned real red when he seen the look on the Judge's as he waited for the insult.

"I mean, Judge. I don't understand what you're doing."

"You don't understand what I'm doing? My, it has been a long time since you practiced law. Why it's simple, Counselor, I'm going to hold a hearing."

LeSeur stared at the Judge like to say he had lost all his marbles. His face twisted up so much I thought it was him that was losing his mind.

LeSeur got mad all over again, and this time it bordered on rage. "A hearing? That's crazy! You can't hold a hearing in a damn cemetery!" he shrieked.

Judge Boudreaux laughed like LeSeur's fly was open and then he talked to him as if LeSeur was a little boy cryin' for his mommy.

"Why not? It's quiet here, certainly. You might have noticed, Counselor, that court observers around here don't have much to say since most of them are dead. In fact, you might say they already had their day in court. It's easy to keep order in such serene surroundings. No, Counselor, this will do just fine."

"Like hell it will! I'll go to the Bar Association!" LeSeur shouted, beside himself.

"Good!" Boudreaux smiled tolerantly at the man, "When do you want to do that? As President of the Bar Association, I'll be glad to accommodate you."

LeSeur scanned the crowd for help or for any sign of encouragement, but saw only hostile stares. He turned back to the Judge, "This is – is – is – "

Judge Boudreaux's expression instantly went from tolerant to a glower that would shrivel a plum into a prune.

"LeSeur, I'll hold you in contempt of court if you say another word."

"There is no court!" LeSeur protested feebly.

"Contempt of cemetery, then! Either way, I'll throw your pompous ass in jail!"

Quickly readjusting, Boudreaux looked around for candidates for other appointments.

"We need a Court Recorder, too."

He pointed at a person in a red and yellow striped costume wearing an enormous ugly head with horns.

"If that's a tape recorder hanging on your shoulder, fella, you're our Court Recorder. If it isn't, go find one."

Judge Boudreaux gestured to one of the cops. "How about y'all go get one of those benches from the walkways and put it at the end of the casket there. We'll use that for the witness box."

The cop hurried away, no doubt glad to get out of the angry stares of Tyrane's mourners.

LeSeur rolled his eyes. "This is craziness," he said. "No one's ever had a hearing in a graveyard."

The Judge ignored him and went on with getting ready to have a hearing.

I hadn't ever been to a hearing, so I got to admit I didn't have no idea what was goin' on. What in the flying flipflop is a hearing?

"We'll need a couple more of those wrought iron seats from the walking path, one of which I'll use as my bench. I'll sit behind the casket, which will do nicely as a desk, quite appropriate, in fact."

When he was satisfied with everything, the Judge took a seat behind Tyrane's casket and started talking like those judges on TV.

"Let's have order in the cemetery now! These proceedings are to determine whether this man—I refer to the one in my desk—" he patted the top of the casket, "may be properly interred in the LeSeur family graveyard next to the late lovely Leona LeSeur in spite of the objections of the senior member of said family, namely, one Edwin LeSeur Jr., who is present in this cemetery and raising objections in the form of loud snorts, profane shouts and occasional statements of disbelief. In other words, he's raising hell."

The judge turned to the man in the horned mask. "Is your tape recorder on?"

"Yes sir, uh, your honor, sir."

A firm and persuasive, but musically pleasant voice came from the onlookers. "Judge Boudreaux, may I approach the casket, I mean bench, sir?"

I turned to see the blonde woman who had come with Ruby Begonia stepping forward. She was tall and good lookin' in a gray suit, and, man, she was all business!

The Judge watched her approach, unsuccessfully hiding his admiration.

"Yes, ma'am, you may approach the casket or bench or anything else you wish, uh, if you have anything you can contribute to these proceedings. First, would you identify yourself to the cemetery … or Court."

She took a business card from her purse, handed it to the Judge and nodded her head at the casket.

"He already knows me," she said softly, and then louder, "My name is Judith Priester. I'm a practicing attorney in Texas, but I am also licensed to practice in this state. The deceased came to the aid of my family when I was quite young and, while it was a long time ago, I feel I should act on behalf of his best friend. If it's acceptable to Felton Haliday and this young man, I would be pleased to represent them in this proceeding. Pro bono, of course."

The Judge looked at Felton and then me.

I looked at Felton with a questioning look but he was too intent watching what was happening to help me. The Judge again looked at Felton and then me.

Felton nodded with a grateful smile and somewhat faraway look on his face. As for me, I didn't have the flyin' foggiest idea what "pro bono" meant. In fact, it sounded kind of like dirty words to me, so I decided to keep my mouth zipped. Felton added, "Me and the boy have no objection, Judge Boudreaux, your honor."

"It's settled then," said the Judge.

LeSeur stepped forward pompously and said irritably, "Judge, you can't allow just anybody to walk into this cemetery."

"Court," the judge corrected with a slight smirk. "Court."

"Oh for Christ's sakes." cried LeSeur, wheeling away disgustedly.

As I watched the Judge, I thought he looked dignified, like a father does, thoughtful and wise, fair and honest, but most of all, like a kind man. Maybe I was seeing him that way 'cause Boudreaux was behind a golden pine casket in which lay a man who had done so much to fill a huge hole in my heart.

It was really weird that, right then and there, I suddenly knew why Tyrane started teaching me to play the fiddle, why he took up so much time with me. I think he knew how missin' my Daddy was eating me up and that the hurt was all bottled up inside me. I don't know how he knew, but he did, and he knew the fiddle would help me bear it.

I felt a tear slide down my cheek. I reached out, put my hand on the pine casket, and whispered, "Thank you, Tyrane."

Judge Boudreaux said to the still furious LeSeur whose lips were stone white, "LeSeur, what testimony do you have to offer this Court to support your claim that these people are trespassers on your family graveyard?"

LeSeur erupted like a volcano spewin' hot lava.

"Testimony? For Christ's sake, Judge, a blind idiot can see they're trespassing and hell, they're making a mockery of my family. I'm the sole heir of Edwin LeSeur, and I'm the executor of the estate. As the patriarch of the LeSeur family, I have every right to deny someone's burial in my family's graveyard."

The Judge's eyes narrowed to slits like old Miss Hurlbutte when she's pissed, only the Judge's was a whole lot meaner. A vein in his forehead swelled up and went to throbbin' and he seemed to be holding himself from smackin' LeSeur on the head.

"Sir, are you prepared to accept the consequences of insulting a Presiding Judge?"

If that Judge was as pissed off at me and stared at me thataway, them eyes shootin' lightning bolts, I'd've curled my butt up like a baby in a corner and went to suckin' my thumb!

LeSeur didn't miss doin' that by too much his self. Boy, you could sure as Jesus tell he was scared plumb to death!

After seeing the look on LeSeur's face, Judge Boudreaux nodded and cooled down.

He said, "I won't require you to provide a copy of your father's will, Mister LeSeur, since I'm sure a copy is on file. In that testament, however, perhaps you could tell the cemetery, uh, court ... Oh, what the hell, cemetery ... what his wishes were regarding the LeSeur grave sites. What did your father have to say about the graveyard itself or this matter specifically?"

"I don't recall. I, uh ..."

Judge Boudreaux said impatiently, "Well, Counselor, he must have made some reference or expressed his desires. Surely you wouldn't be jumping up and down and raving like a lunatic over this matter if there was no mention of it in his probated will. What did he say? What were his wishes?"

"Hell, Judge, the graveyard is property of the estate. He didn't refer to it directly in the will."

LeSeur looked confused, and he sure didn't like where this was going.

The Judge raised his eyebrows significantly, waved his hand to say it didn't matter none, and said, "All right, Counselor. That's fine. That will be all. Counselor Priester, am I to understand that you have something you wish to contribute to this Cemetery Hearing?"

I thought, "Cemetery Hearing." It looked like the Judge had done give a legal name to this whole thing.

The Priester woman stepped to the right of the casket, smiled at everybody and replied, "Yes, sir, I have much to offer this cemetery hearing. I think we can clear up some of the questions. I'd like to interrogate a witness. May I ask young Eldridge Brewer to come up? He's my first witness."

Lord, I was scared. My belly did a flipflop like when Miss Hurlbutte caught me 'n Peepee tryin' out cigarettes behind the gym last month. I was tryin' my best to understand what was goin' on, but they was using words I ain't never. I hoped "interrogate" didn't mean stickin' needles in me.

Here was a real Judge who was more important than anybody I ever been this close to. He even talked like he had read all the legal books ever writ in the world. LeSeur was about to mess his pants and now here was a woman lawyer who seemed more powerful than Mother Nature!

And, holy pumpkin pie, I was a witness!

I stood up, forgetting about my ankle and almost fell down. I caught myself and managed to limp to the lawn bench they put by the casket. Each step hurt like the devil.

While I made my way, Lieutenant Custer leaned over to the Judge and spent several seconds talking low into his ear, all the while looking hard at me as if I was a serial killer or something worse, like another lawyer. Leastways, I could tell he wasn't telling the Judge that I was his idea of a righteous altar boy.

CHAPTER SEVENTEEN

Judge Boudreaux nodded at whatever the cop told him and then said, "Reverend Briox, you may swear in the witness."

LeSeur rolled his eyes in disgust and muttered, "I'm not believing this."

The preacher was almost overcome with everything that was goin' on. You could tell he ain't never been a Clerk of Court, which I reckon he thought was lots more important than preachin' the gospel.

"Yes, Sir. Right away your honorable sir."

He run up to me and stuck a Bible out at me. "Master, uh ..."

"Eldy. I mean, I'm Eldridge Brewer, sir," I said.

He was so up tight he couldn't remember his own name much less the name of some smarty-ass kid like me.

"Master Brewer, yes, of course. Place your right hand on the Lord's Testament."

I did, and he started like we was standing before the throne of the Almighty and he was presenting me as a sacrifice.

"Do you, Eldridge Brewer, accept Jesus as your Lord and Savior? If so, answer—"

"Reverend," Judge Boudreaux interrupted impatiently, "we're not conferring sainthood here. Just hold the Bible for him, okay?"

Face red with embarrassment, preacher Briox defended himself, "I was just being thorough, your honor."

"We don't need thorough, Preacher. Hold the Bible."

The judge said to me with a smile, "You swear to tell the truth, son?"

"Yes, sir, your honorship."

He kept the smile, but it had something hard in it too.

"What happened to your ankle?"

I looked across at Bella who stood by Mama. She smiled at me and I thought, why am I so scared? I didn't do nothing wrong. Them bikers might call me a juvenile delinquent, but they'd be full of it.

I didn't look him square in the eye when I replied.

"I jumped from too high up and sprained my ankle, sir, I mean, your honorship."

The judge seemed to be thinking about something. My face started to burn as he looked at me.

After a while, he said, "If I asked you if you knew anything about that hot air balloon going off yonder—the one you can barely see now, with the motorcycles hanging from it—would you tell me the truth?"

All right, I done some mischief. It was me put the opossum in Miss Hurlbutte's desk drawer and I put the chicken snake in Uncle Felix's car at the Fourth of July picnic. I didn't know he'd get so bamfoozled, he'd drive into the Moonshine Memorial Lake. And okay, it was me put that chipmunk in the mailman's mailbag whilst he wasn't looking. But, oh Lordy, help me now, I ain't never fell in the hole of a two seater outhouse like I have today!

I was scared, but I knew I wouldn't lie about it 'ceptin' to keep Bella out of it. I looked down and mumbled, "Y–yes, sir." Here it comes.

He waited for me to look up and studied me for a long second, staring into my eyes. Finally, he nodded, smiled and said, "Yes, I believe you would. Good! That's what I would ask you about, if that was the matter at hand. However, that is not the issue we are dealing with today."

He stared hard at LeSeur and his biker driver, and added with a warning in his voice, "I'll insist on adjudicating it myself if it ever comes up."

That last sounded scary, but not as much for me as for LeSeur.

"Now, Master Brewer, tell this cemetery how it is that you and Mr. Haliday drove the deceased all the way here from West Virginia to be interred next to Leona LeSeur."

I wasn't sure what "interred" meant, but I took a deep breath and told him about the cigar box full of love letters, the letter from Leona's father, and Felton turning up on the day Tyrane Percival died.

"So the three of us put Tyrane in Felton's pickup truck and brought him here even though some bikers tried to stop us in Alabama ..."

The judge raised his hand. "The three of you?"

"Yes sir. Whistler came too. We didn't know he was in the truck 'til we done got too far to go back."

"And Whistler is?"

"The dog yonder," I answered, pointing at Whistler who had selected a cool spot by Punky and was grinning at me, "That's Tyrane's dog, your honorship. He farts in e-flat, although sometimes it's a b-flat. Anyway, He's named for his farts."

Everybody was quiet up till then, but after me tellin' about Whistler's farts and all, they like to have fell down laughing.

Judge Boudreaux's face was stern, but with a twinkle in his eye, he allowed the laughter for a few seconds before he pulled a wooden hammer from his coat and pounded Tyrane's casket.

"Order! Order in the cemetery!" he hollered.

The crowd shut up like kids caught talkin' in the library, and I was just able to hear the Judge whisper at the casket, "Sorry, Ty."

He cleared his throat and turned to Felton.

"This letter, Mister Haliday. Do you have it with you?"

"Yes, your honor. It's in the Studebaker."

"Please, get it for us."

"Yes sir."

Felton hurried to the truck, and brought the cigar box back to the football helmet and handed it to Judge Boudreaux.

"The letter is on top."

Judge Boudreaux opened the box and took out the top piece of paper.

With a solemn, sad expression on his face, he flicked his fingers through the sheaf of love letters, and then unfolded the letter and read it aloud.

His courtroom ways and great big voice made everybody shut up and listen. It got quiet the way it does when a judge reads the verdict in a big murder trial. When he finished, he took off his glasses and fingered his eye. He made like something got in it, but I'm too sharp for that. I knew it was a tear.

Aunt Bessie started to cry and, remembering the pile of 'em on our kitchen table, I knew we didn't have enough paper towels for her, much less for everybody else in the football helmet wiping their eyes.

Edwin LeSeur's face was all twisted up, and I could tell his feelings was mixed up, all jumbled together and fighting one another. I think there was an awful bitterness driving him that we didn't know nothin' about. I can't say how I knew it, but I knew didn't none of us cause what was eatin' him up. He was taking it out on us as a way to make his own pain go away.

I suddenly understood Edwin LeSeur. He was hurtin' something awful, like you hurt when you lose something real, real, real precious.

I ain't but twelve, but I know how hard it is to hurt like that, 'cause I hurt like that about my Daddy till the other night.

It's like a dirty cut on your finger gets red and infected and the pus is making the hurt mean and ugly. It was like that for me until I let myself cry about it—let it out, you know. I miss my Daddy just like always, but it don't hurt no more, not like it did.

I think LeSeur heard his own father's words squeeze the infection from his soul. It was like all that meanness—that pus—went out of him, and although he objected, his earlier ranting and raving was gone.

He said, "I object. I don't know whether that letter was really by … you know … maybe he didn't …"

"I have another witness, your Honor." Judith Priester interrupted. "I think she can shed some light on this matter and certainly confirm the authorship of that letter."

She motioned to the little old lady I had noticed earlier.

She had a cane and moved very slowly, picking her way as if the ground was covered with broken Christmas balls. I was so busy watching her that I almost missed hearing Edwin LeSeur suck in his breath like he seen a ghost.

LeSeur stared at the little old lady like he didn't believe his eyes.

"Oh, my God. Aunt Leona!"

"Yes, Junior, your Aunt Leona."

Her voice was all shaky and weak, but she sounded like she was ready to fight, and her face was clear and strong.

"This nice lady was kind enough to pick me up at the home that you so seldom find time to visit."

LeSeur's face was scarlet.

"Aunt Leona, I … I …"

Priester said, "Judge Boudreaux, this is Leona Baxter, the late Edwin LeSeur's sister. I only learned about her recently."

Turning to the Judge, Leona Baxter, said, "The letter is genuine, Judge Boudreaux. I was with my brother a great deal of the time in his final days. He wrote that letter with my help, and I can tell you he will rest better knowing a wrong he committed has been made right, if Tyrane Percival is buried next to his only daughter. She was named after me, and I loved her as if she was the daughter I never had."

Then she turned to Edwin LeSeur.

"You were a disappointment to your father, Edwin, for so much of his life. Can't you, for at least this once, do what he wanted? You resented Tyrane for no other reason than pure jealousy."

She looked off a moment and then back at LeSeur.

"Today, right now, you can prove that you're as good a man as Tyrane was. Not only that, you can show a respect for your sister in death that you never showed her or your father when they were alive."

I ain't got words enough to tell you about the look on LeSeur's face. He was embarrassed, I could see that. Pain was there too, a lot of it. But most of all, I think he was ashamed. I think that shame had eaten away all the best things in him and he knew it.

It's not enough to say he was speechless, or that he couldn't make words with his tongue and mouth. It was as if he had turned in on himself.

Edwin LeSeur Jr., looked like poor Peepee did when a Bickford street kid won all his marbles, only a lot worse. He looked as if his life had got so rotten that he couldn't live it no more. Tears welled in his eyes and his lips trembled.

Finally he barely mumbled, "I … I'm sorry, Aunt Leona. I don't know …"

The man's hurt hung on his face, naked and terrible for all of us to see.

I suddenly felt all that anger at him leave me like a fog burned off by the sun. One minute I wanted to stink up his limo with Whistler, and the next minute, I didn't want to add to his pain. I felt sorry for Edwin LeSeur because I understood.

Edwin LeSeur's loss of a sister and then his father while they was pissed off at one another hurt him so much that he had to cause pain for others so that the pain in his own heart wouldn't hurt so much.

That might not make sense to anybody else, but that's sure as hell what I thought watching Edwin LeSeur, and I knew I was right, like when I get the sweet spot of my bat on a fastball.

I don't know what made me speak up at that moment. I've often wondered if maybe Tyrane reached out of his pine casket and took me over like a ghost.

"Mr. LeSeur," I said, "I was going to put Tyrane's cigar box with the love letters him and your sister wrote to one another on the casket, you know, so they could read them to each other, uh, up there." I jerked my chin up toward the sky.

LeSeur stared at me. His eyes were red and full of tears.

I looked around at everybody, at Mama, Sarah Bella, and finally at Felton. He seemed to read my mind and nodded like to say "go ahead."

"It would please me and all of us here," I went on, "and I bet Tyrane too, for you to do that, if you've a mind to."

The Judge offered no resistance when I took the box from him and handed it to LeSeur.

He stared at it for a moment, then at me, and then took it. His hands trembled as he held it.

"You would do that after everything I've done to you and Felton?" He asked.

"Yes, sir, I sure would."

I can't explain this at all, but I never felt as right about something as I did about Edwin LeSeur putting that box on Tyrane's casket. Tyrane taught me how to play the fiddle, but I knew right then standing under that football helmet that he taught me a whole lot more than that.

Turning to Felton and the others, he said, "Felton, I don't know what to say. I ..."

"Edwin," Felton said, "I think Tyrane Percival wanted us to lay him to rest beside Leona, but I think he also wanted the bitterness that racked your family to end. Somehow he used this boy and his estranged best friend to make that happen. I'm not going to question it. I'm just gonna go with it and add my invitation to that of my partner, Eldridge Brewer."

Felton patted LeSeur's shoulder.

"You place the box."

The only sound in the cemetery was the soft panting of Whistler. Edwin LeSeur stepped up to the casket. His hands shook as he put the cigar box in the center of the flowers.

"Tyrane," holding back sobs, he began, "Daddy told me he was writing the letter. When I found out, I went a little crazy, said some awful things.

Daddy and I didn't speak after that, and then one day it was too late. He was gone. I blamed you, because I couldn't live with my own shame. I'll pray the rest of my life that you and Leona will forgive me."

I know everybody there must have thought about how they had treated somebody special before they died and I bet a lot of 'em went home thinking about it.

After what seemed forever, Judge Boudreaux announced, "Well, it seems this hearing is over, and we can now have a proper burial of Tyrane Percival. Rev. Briox, you are relieved as cemetery clerk and can resume your role as presiding preacher. He banged his courtroom hammer again and said under his breath, "Sorry again, Ty."

The ceremony went on slick as a greased pig after that. Reverend Briox preached so long that when Whistler stopped it with a world-class punctuation of one of the Reverend's most important amens, everybody was grateful, notwithstanding having to gasp for clean air. We were lucky, though, that a gust of wind relieved most of us from having to live with it for too long.

Many of the mourners drifted away while attendants got the grave ready for viewing, but those closest to the events of the day stayed, along with some early members of the Funshiners. Edwin LeSeur stayed quite a while and would have stayed longer, I think, 'ceptin' his Aunt Leona got real tired, and he took her back to the home.

Felton and I stood apart from the rest, while Mama and Aunt Bessie visited with people, learning about the adventures of the Funshiners.

Felton said, "Well, Eldy, we did it. I don't know how, but we did it."

"Tyrane did it, I think." I said.

"Out of the mouths of babes."

"Now, what does that mean?" I said glaring at him.

"Nothing."

The lawyer lady came up and gave Felton a big hug.

He said, "I can't believe what a lovely and capable woman you have grown into, Squirt."

"I'm not a squirt any more, Mister Haliday," she replied with a light and airy laugh. She thought a minute. "You know, if Tyrane hadn't helped us, I don't know what would have happened."

Reverend Briox touched Felton on the arm. "It's ready, Mister Haliday," he said.

We all turned to see that the grave was filled in, a green cover that looked like grass put over it, and the flowers neatly arranged.

We planned to tell Mr. Tweedleman to put on the tombstone:

Tyrane Percival

1926 – 1989

He Loved Leona

Everyone gathered around Felton and me. Chief Wampooti pressed something into my hand. It was Tyrane's fiddle. Judge Boudreaux's driver arrived at his side with a bass, and the circuit Judge smiled his appreciation.

At the same time, Sol Goldstein handed Felton the package he had been carrying.

"I didn't recognize it until I looked at the neck and saw 'Banjo' carved there. I believe this is yours."

Felton Haliday's mouth gaped open as he took the banjo from Sol.

"It's ... it's really mine. How did ...?"

He stared at Goldstein.

"Just lucky, I guess. Can you still play?"

"I don't know, Sol. It's been a long time."

"He can still play," I piped up confidently. I nocked the fiddle under my chin, turned to Felton and said, "You said you wouldn't play again until you could play for Tyrane and Leona together." I drew the bow across the strings gently, persuasively. "Well, here it is, Felton. They're together."

As if it was prearranged, Judge Boudreaux began strumming the bass in a sweet rhythm for "Blue Eyes Cryin' in the Rain." Felton, hesitant at first, strummed a little, and then as if some spirit had entered his soul, that banjo came alive as no musical instrument ever had before.

Epilogue

I closed the manuscript and became suddenly aware of my surroundings, of the sights, sounds and smells of a great venue in Boston, Massachusetts. It had been so long since I read the story I wrote when I was young and, I suppose some would say foolish, that I was hearing again the sounds of yesteryear.

No group ever played a song with as much reverence as we did so long ago on that memorable day in the Shady Rest Cemetery, or played hymns of joy and release during the return procession with more exuberance. Tyrane's mourners danced all the way back to the bandstand in the park where a contemporary Funshiners band played and sang into the night. We made the delightful discovery that Judith Priester, the little girl from that family Ty had helped so long ago, could sing like a bird.

The hot air balloon came down that afternoon in Lake Ponchartrain near New Orleans miraculously undamaged. The motorcycles are probably still at the bottom of the lake, but the bikers decided discretion was the better part of valor and slunk back to wherever they came from. I never really knew how I didn't get in serious trouble over the balloon, but if I had to guess, Chief Wampooti and Judge Boudreaux probably had a lot to do with it. I can still hear the Chief's answer when I asked about it. "Great Chickasaw spirit move in mysterious ways. Make trouble go away."

Someone tapped on the door.

The door opened and a man stuck his head in. Over his shoulder, I could clearly see the cavernous auditorium behind him and the house lights flash on the instruments of the Boston Pops Orchestra.

"Ten minutes, Mister Brewer. It's the hottest ticket in town, sir. Looks like a full house again."

I smiled at him and asked, "Did you get Bella and the kids seated?"

"Yes, sir. They're sitting in the VIP balcony box on the right. Your mother and father are there, too."

"Thank you, I'll be right out."

It didn't seem important to explain that Felton was actually my stepfather, a technicality anyway.

I thought about the program for tonight and about what I would say to explain the closing number. It would be impossible to tell the story. Who would care anyway? I would just tell them that the song was very special to my family and me, which would give me a chance to acknowledge them.

Accompanying orchestras used to question closing on such a sad song, but they don't anymore, especially since I require it in the contract for my appearances.

It's probably silly, but I've always felt that Tyrane and Leona could hear it and understand. As I started out of the wings onto the vast stage, the applause grew into a great crescendo and I knew Tyrane could hear that, too.

About the author

Red Evans

From his first years as a radio personality to respected television journalist, to Washington activist and entertaining public speaker, Andreas W. (Red) Evans' writing has turned up in the Congressional Record, the nation's largest newspapers and now in this delightful novel. He is a fourth generation native of Charleston, South Carolina whose great grandfather served as mayor of the historic city in the nineteenth century. Red's multiple careers have taken him all over the world. In the Nation's Capital he produced the widely read *The Federal Employee*, the oldest newspaper of its genre in the U.S.

Now retired in Mt. Pleasant, S.C. with his wife, Marie and Shih Tzu, Buster, Red is enjoying watching the maturation of his grandchildren, "and having the time of my life writing and telling stories, some true and some, well ..."

KÜNATI

Provocative. Bold. Controversial.

Kunati Fall 2007 titles

Available at your favorite bookseller

www.kunati.com

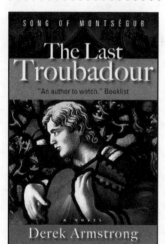

The Last Troubadour
Historical fiction by Derek Armstrong

Against the flames of a rising medieval Inquisition, a heretic, an atheist and a pagan are the last hope to save the holiest Christian relic from a sainted king and crusading pope. Based on true events.
■ "A series to watch ... Armstrong injects the trope with new vigor." *Booklist*

US\$ 24.95 | Pages 384, cloth hardcover
ISBN-13: 978-1-60164-010-9
ISBN-10: 1-60164-010-2
EAN: 9781601640109

Recycling Jimmy
A cheeky, outrageous novel by Andy Tilley

Two Manchester lads mine a local hospital ward for "clients" as they launch Quitters, their suicide-for-profit venture in this off-the-wall look at death and modern life.

US\$ 24.95 | Pages 256, cloth hardcover
ISBN-13: 978-1-60164-013-0
ISBN-10: 1-60164-013-7
EAN 9781601640130

Women Of Magdalene
A hauntingly tragic tale of the old South by Rosemary Poole-Carter

An idealistic young doctor in the post-Civil War South exposes the greed and cruelty at the heart of the Magdalene Ladies' Asylum in this elegant, richly detailed and moving story of love and sacrifice.

US$ 24.95 | Pages 288, cloth hardcover
ISBN-13: 978-1-60164-014-7
ISBN-10: 1-60164-014-5
EAN: 9781601640147

On Ice
A road story like no other, by Red Evans

The sudden death of a sad old fiddle player brings new happiness and hope to those who loved him in this charming, earthy, hilarious coming-of-age tale.

US$ 19.95 | Pages 208, cloth hardcover
ISBN-13: 978-1-60164-015-4
ISBN-10: 1-60164-015-3
EAN: 9781601640154

Truth Or Bare
Offbeat, stylish crime novel by Richard Cahill

The characters throb with vitality, the prose sizzles in this darkly comic page-turner set in the sleazy world of murderous sex workers, the justice system, and the rich who will stop at nothing to get what they want.

US$ 24.95 | Pages 304, cloth hardcover
ISBN-13: 978-1-60164-016-1
ISBN-10: 1-60164-016-1
EAN: 9781601640161

Provocative. Bold. Controversial.

The Game
A thriller by Derek Armstrong

Reality television becomes too real when a killer stalks the cast on America's number one live-broadcast reality show.
■ "A series to watch ... Armstrong injects the trope with new vigor." *Booklist*
US$ 24.95 | Pages 352, cloth hardcover
ISBN 978-1-60164-001-7 | EAN: 9781601640017
LCCN 2006930183

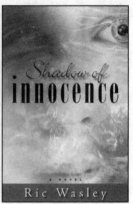

bang BANG
A novel by Lynn Hoffman

In Lynn Hoffman's wickedly funny *bang-BANG*, a waitress crime victim takes on America's obsession with guns and transforms herself in the process. Read along as Paula becomes national hero and villain, enforcer and outlaw, lover and leader. Don't miss Paula Sherman's one-woman quest to change America.
■ "Brilliant"
STARRED REVIEW, *Booklist*
US$ 19.95
Pages 176, cloth hardcover
ISBN 978-1-60164-000-0
EAN 9781601640000
LCCN 2006930182

Whale Song
A novel by Cheryl Kaye Tardif

Whale Song is a haunting tale of change and choice. Cheryl Kaye Tardif's beloved novel—a "wonderful novel that will make a wonderful movie" according to *Writer's Digest*—asks the difficult question, which is the higher morality, love or law?
■ "Crowd-pleasing ... a big hit." *Booklist*
US$ 12.95
Pages 208, UNA trade paper
ISBN 978-1-60164-007-9
EAN 9781601640079
LCCN 2006930188

Shadow of Innocence
A mystery by Ric Wasley

The Thin Man meets *Pulp Fiction* in a unique mystery set amid the drugs-and-music scene of the sixties that touches on all our societal taboos. *Shadow of Innocence* has it all: adventure, sleuthing, drugs, sex, music and a perverse shadowy secret that threatens to tear apart a posh New England town.
US$ 24.95
Pages 304, cloth hardcover
ISBN 978-1-60164-006-2
EAN 9781601640062
LCCN 2006930187

The Secret Ever Keeps
A novel by Art Tirrell

An aging Godfather-like billionaire tycoon regrets a decades-long life of "shady dealings" and seeks reconciliation with a granddaughter who doesn't even know he exists. A sweeping adventure across decades—from Prohibition to today—exploring themes of guilt, greed and forgiveness.

■ "Riveting ... Rhapsodic ... Accomplished." *ForeWord*

US$ 24.95
Pages 352, cloth hardcover
ISBN 978-1-60164-004-8
EAN 9781601640048
LCCN 2006930185

Toonamint of Champions
A wickedly allegorical comedy by Todd Sentell

Todd Sentell pulls out all the stops in his hilarious spoof of the manners and mores of America's most prestigious golf club. A cast of unforgettable characters, speaking a language only a true son of the South could pull off, reveal that behind the gates of fancy private golf clubs lurk some mighty influential freaks.

■ "Bubbly imagination and wacky humor." *ForeWord*

US$ 19.95
Pages 192, cloth hardcover
ISBN 978-1-60164-005-5
EAN 9781601640055
LCCN 2006930186

Mothering Mother
A daughter's humorous and heartbreaking memoir.
Carol D. O'Dell

Mothering Mother is an authentic, "in-the-room" view of a daughter's struggle to care for a dying parent. It will touch you and never leave you.

■ "Beautiful, told with humor... and much love." *Booklist*

■ "I not only loved it, I lived it. I laughed, I smiled and shuddered reading this book." Judith H. Wright, author of over 20 books.

US$ 19.95
Pages 208, cloth hardcover
ISBN 978-1-60164-003-1
EAN 9781601640031
LCCN 2006930184

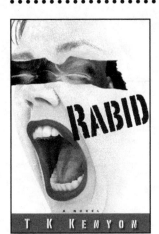

Rabid
A novel by T K Kenyon

A sexy, savvy, darkly funny tale of ambition, scandal, forbidden love and murder. Nothing is sacred. The graduate student, her professor, his wife, her priest: four brilliantly realized characters spin out of control in a world where science and religion are in constant conflict.

■ "Kenyon is definitely a keeper." STARRED REVIEW, *Booklist*

US$ 26.95 | Pages 480, cloth hardcover
ISBN 978-1-60164-002-4 | EAN: 9781601640024
LCCN 2006930189